YOU DID WHAT??!

BOOKS BY TRISTAN BANCKS

My Life and Other Stuff I Made Up
My Life and Other Stuff that Went Wrong
My Life and Other Massive Mistakes

Two Wolves

Mac Slater 1: The Rules of Cool
Mac Slater 2: I ❤ NY

MY LiFE

& other Massive Mistakes

Tristan Bancks

pics by gus gordon

RANDOM HOUSE AUSTRALIA

Tristan Bancks is an ambassador for
Room to Read. Find out more at:
www.roomtoread.org/australia

A Random House book
Published by Random House Australia Pty Ltd
Level 3, 100 Pacific Highway, North Sydney NSW 2060
www.randomhouse.com.au

Penguin
Random House
RANDOM HOUSE BOOKS

First published by Random House Australia in 2015

Text copyright © Tristan Bancks 2015
Illustration copyright © Gus Gordon 2015

The moral right of the author and illustrator has been asserted.

Random House Books is part of the Penguin Random House group of
companies whose addresses can be found at global.penguinrandomhouse.com.

National Library of Australia
Cataloguing-in-Publication Entry

    Author: Bancks, Tristan
    Title: My life and other massive mistakes/Tristan Bancks; illustrated
    by Gus Gordon
    ISBN: 978 0 85798 529 3 (paperback)
    Series: Bancks, Tristan. My life; 3
    Target Audience: For primary school age
    Other Authors/Contributors: Gordon, Gus, illustrator
    Dewey Number: A823.4

Cover and internal illustrations by Gus Gordon
Cover and internal design by Astred Hicks, designcherry.com
Printed in Australia by Griffin Press, an accredited ISO AS/NZS 14001:2004
Environmental Management System printer

Random House Australia uses papers that are natural, renewable and
recyclable products and made from wood grown in sustainable forests.
The logging and manufacturing processes are expected to conform to the
environmental regulations of the country of origin.

Contents

Hey,

I'm Tom Weekly and this is my life. Every single word in this book is true. Except the stuff I made up.

See, I have trouble working out where reality stops and fantasy begins. Tanya, my evil-genius criminal-mastermind sister, says that makes me a liar. But that's not true. Stella Holling really *did* try to trick me into kissing her on her chocolate-smothered lips. I actually *did* help my pop attempt a breakout from Kings Bay Nursing Home. And, yes, I *did* try to use Lewis Snow's nits as a biological weapon to shut down my school.

If you have any weird, funny or gross stories, jokes or drawings you'd like me to put into my next book or on my website, I'm at:

TheTomWeekly@gmail.com

Be kind to your nits. (And Lewis
says try feeding them small dollops
of tomato sauce. It's their second
favourite food, after blood.)

Tom

NitPlan

I plunge my arm deep into the forest of Lewis Snow's hair and scrape my fingernails across his scalp. When I withdraw my hand it is crawling, teeming, *seething* with head lice.

'I dunno if this is the epic-est thing I've ever seen or if I'm going to vomit,' I whisper to Lewis and Jack.

'Maybe both,' Lewis replies with a smile.

There aren't just dozens of nits on Lewis's scalp. Or hundreds. There are *thousands*. Tens of thousands, maybe. It doesn't even seem possible that this many nits exist in the world, let alone on one very small head.

'Just don't hurt them,' Lewis says. 'Nits are people, too.'

Lewis has had nits since he was three years old. He reckons he can't remember *not* having an itchy head. He's had nits for so long he sees them as pets. He reckons they speak to him, that all his best ideas come from his nits. Lewis was expelled from his last school for having too many nits, but our school will take anybody.

I proceed to release the minibeasts into the wild, depositing 50 to 100 extra-large nits into each blue hat on each peg outside each classroom in the main school corridor. We even get the teachers' hats. All the other kids are in assembly so the place is deserted, apart from me, Jack and Lewis. And the nits.

'Pace yourselves,' Jack whispers, delving his own hand into Lewis's wild blond afro. 'We've still got a bunch of classes to do.'

'It's okay,' Lewis replies. 'Plenty to go round.'

Jack and I continue to spread the nit love until we make it to the end of the very long corridor. We look back. Hundreds of blue school hats are wriggling with lice.

'Good job, men,' Jack whispers. 'Only our class left to do.'

'Four minutes,' Lewis confirms, checking the timer on his watch, which is in sync with the school bell.

Just enough time to finish sowing the seeds of our terrible plan: complete school shutdown before next week's dreaded national standardised tests, when we face the hardest exams of our lives.

Jack, Lewis and I reckon that our talents

can't be measured by a test. So we figure that
if there were, say, a plague of head lice and
every kid in school had to be sent home . . .

Boom.

No exams.

We've been hatching the plan for three
weeks. The idea came to us on the day that
Lewis Snow, the kid with the worst case of
nits in world history – Jack's and my new
best friend and hero – wandered into our
classroom, scratching like mad.

Lewis, Jack and I slip into three empty seats
at the back of assembly next to a sleeping Mr
Carter, just as the recess bell sounds.

'STAY in your seats!' Mr Skroop demands
from centre stage. He seems to be staring
right through me with those charcoal eyes.
Walton Skroop is not my biggest fan, which
is unlucky because he recently landed the job

of deputy principal. And he's my next-door neighbour.

'As you know, we have examinations next week and I expect you all to be using your preparation time wisely. The reputation of this school, our funding and even your teachers' jobs depend on these results. I will be very, *very* disappointed if we do poorly. Do you understand?'

'Yes, Mr Skroop,' we all say in unison.

'Now please leave the hall in a *calm and orderly fashion*, one class at a time, beginning with 6A!'

We slowly file out of the hall, across the playground and into the main school building, where everyone grabs their food and hats for recess. Jack, Lewis and I stand at the end of the corridor, near the library, watching as our scheme unfolds.

'I love it when a plan comes together,' I say.

'We are great humanitarians,' Jack agrees.

'I love nits,' Lewis says dreamily.

By the afternoon everyone is scratching.

Everyone.

Kindergarten kids, primary kids, teachers – even Mr Barnes, the maintenance guy.

'*Please* stop scratching and concentrate on your work,' Miss Norrish snips. 'You heard what Mr Skroop said this morning.'

We are at our desks doing last year's maths test, preparing for next week's exam. Apart from Jack, everyone around me is scratching. Miss Norrish is up the front, marking papers. She's usually calm and fun, but today she's on edge. I think she's as scared of Mr Skroop as we are.

'Excuse me,' Raph Atkins says.

'Yes, Raph.'

'I'm itchy.'

'Just ignore it,' Miss Norrish snaps.

'But it feels like my head's about to explode.'

'I will make it explode if you don't stop scratching.'

'I think I have zombie nits,' he says.

SLAM!

Miss Norrish throws a textbook down on her desk, stands and says, 'This is ridiculous. I don't know what's got into you all this afternoon.'

'I'm itchy,' a small voice says at the back.

'I know that! So am I!' Miss Norrish shouts and then scratches her head like a wild woman, turning her usually dead-straight hair into a haystack. 'Get out, all of you! Go outside and scratch yourselves silly. Go on, GO!'

At first we're not sure if she's serious, but eventually we head out into the playground.

'This is awesome,' Jack whispers.

miss Norrish's nits are
nicely nourished.

The next two days whirl by in a storm
of school-wide scratching and teacher
meltdowns, but it's Friday before the nits really
hit the fan. Jack, Lewis and I skate to school
together. As we roll through the top gates, we
stop and stare.

'What's happening?' I ask.

'I dunno,' Jack says.

'My nits have a bad feeling about this,' Lewis mutters.

There is a queue of about 40 parents on the stairs leading up to the front office. All the kids in the playground are being rounded up by teachers and marched towards the hall.

'The bell hasn't even gone,' Jack says.

We pick up our skateboards and walk down the driveway. Pretty soon, we are swept up in the tidal wave of kids pouring into the hall.

Inside, everyone is lined around the walls in class groups, scratching. Kindergarten is up near the stage. Years one and two are against the side wall and year three is at the back. The line-up of kids wraps right around to year six at the front of the hall again, under the basketball backboard. Lewis, Jack and I take our places.

Mr Skroop stands in the centre of the hall with a microphone. Even from this distance his brown, gappy teeth and fluorescent white skin make me shiver.

'*This*,' Mr Skroop begins as the last few kids straggle in, 'is a great *in*convenience.'

He turns slowly to look at each and every child, his eyes boring into us.

'*This*,' he goes on, 'is a source of great antagonism and *frustration* for me. *Someone* in

I think our school HAS a nit problem...

this room is responsible for the unprecedented outbreak of *Pediculus humanus capitis*, commonly known as head lice.'

How could he know? I wonder. *How could he know the nits didn't just* naturally *invade the school?*

'*You,*' he says, 'know who you are.'

Lewis's leg is shaking. I can see it out of the corner of my eye. I don't look at his face. Jack picks the scab on his nose. He does that when he's nervous. I remember the time I was in hospital and Mr Skroop ate Jack's knee-scab. I'm still annoyed with him about that. It was the biggest in my collection.

'I have had some very unhappy parents in my office this morning,' he says, 'and when I have unhappy parents in my office, that makes *me* unhappy and when *I* am unhappy, that means *you* should be unhappy, too, because *I* am the captain of this ship.'

Lewis's leg is really jittering now. And Jack's nose is bleeding. Kids all around whisper nervously to one another.

'SILENCE!' Mr Skroop howls. Four hundred kids and 12 teachers snap to attention. He slithers towards the kindergarten kids, just to my left. He's so close that I can smell the stink of his beastly cat, Mr Fatterkins, on his shredded maroon jumper.

The kindy kids cower before Dark Lord Skroop as he walks by. A blond boy wets himself. Mrs Rodgers lifts him out of the puddle and helps him over to the side doors.

Mr Skroop continues around the large rectangle of fear, past each and every child. He regards them with deep suspicion before moving on. The only sounds are the ominous clops of Skroop's footsteps and the constant *shooka-shooka-shooka* of head scratching. Skroop examines first grade, second grade, third grade.

'The nits think we should confess,' Lewis says.

I shush him. 'Just act normal.' But it's hard to act normal when you're trying to act normal. You keep thinking, *Just act normal, just act normal*, until you don't even know what the word 'normal' means anymore.

Mr Skroop stops and stares at a fourth grader until the kid starts bawling. He passes the halfway line on the basketball court, moving towards us. My bladder is bulging at the seams. I hope I don't end up in a puddle, too.

Just act normal, just act normal, just act normal.

Skroop is ten metres away and he still hasn't bagged the culprit. Why isn't he stopping? Why doesn't he suspect any of these kids? What about Jonah Flem? What about Brent Bunder? How suspicious do those guys look? They're about the most suspicious-looking guys I've ever seen. They would steal an old lady's porridge faster than they'd help her across the street. They rip the wings off flies for fun. They almost have moustaches. They should be in high school already. They –

He's here.

Skroop.

Walton Skroop.

He looks deeply into Lewis's eyes and even more deeply into mine. I can't look away. His stare is a straw, reaching in through my eyes to suck out my soul. Skroop sniffs. He can smell

the lies seeping from my skin, I'm sure of it.
I reek of fibs. I am a wanted criminal and this
is the end of the line. I'll be
expelled and my mum will send
me to Brat Camp, where we'll
be the stars of a reality TV series
and people all over the world
will know me as the Nit Bandit,
the kid who used head lice as a
biological weapon to shut down
his school. Maybe Lewis's nits
are right – we need to fess up
now. Criminals on TV always
get off lighter when they admit
they're guilty. I open my mouth,
ready to confess . . .

He moves on.

He takes a quick look at Jack
and says, 'Your scab is bleeding.
Get yourself a bandaid.' Then
he walks past.

GREAT
humaNiTarians
in History

nit

Gone.

It's over.

We're off the hook.

Free as birds.

Total school shutdown before Monday's exams becomes a real possibility once more. I try not to smile. Lewis's leg stops shaking so badly. Jack dabs at the blood on his nose with a tissue. I can breathe again. I feel good. Mum always tells me I'm a worrywart, and I guess I am. I really am. I had noth–

Mr Skroop stops and looks back over his shoulder at us. At me. But I'm not worried because I don't feel so guilty anymore. I feel relaxed. I give him a pursed-lip smile that tells him just how seriously I'm taking this and that I know how hard it must be for teachers to have scallywags like these nit bandits on the loose.

Skroop turns, tilts his head to the side slightly and sniffs the air again like a dog considering attack. His dead-black eyes are trained on us. I must admit, I do feel a little nervous again.

Jack whispers, 'Oh no,' in my ear and I whisper, 'Shhh!' without moving my lips. I do it pretty well. I decide that if I make it out of this alive I might become a ventriloquist.

Skroop slides back towards us. The entire school looks on. Fire burns behind his eyes. He stops in front of me. He is the Voldemort to my Harry. I'm pretty sure I can see a drop of unicorn blood at the corner of his mouth.

Lewis's leg starts dancing again.

'Look around the hall,' Skroop says, keeping his eyes locked on me.

I look around.

'What do you see?' he asks.

'K-kids,' I say.

'And what are they *doing*?'

This feels like a trick question. They just seem to be standing there but I don't want to say, 'Standing there,' because he'll think that I'm trying to be smart. See, I know how teachers' minds work. But the kids really do appear to just be standing there.

'Um . . . Standing there?' I offer.

'What else?' he says, stretching the 's' on 'else' as though he might be part snake.

I look around. I feel like the exams have started early. I wish it were multiple choice. I have no idea what he wants to hear. After a long time he snaps, 'They are *scratching*, you imbecile. Don't you see?'

I look around. And I do see. They *are* scratching. All of them.

'But you and your little friend here –' he looks at Jack '– are not. Tell me why.'

'Um.' I can't believe we forgot to scratch. *Just act normal, just act normal.*

'Is it because,' Skroop asks, 'for some reason, you were not infected with head lice while every other child and teacher in the school was?' He scratches his head just behind the ear.

'I saw the two of you – and the new boy here, with the ridiculous hair – slip into the back of this week's school assembly late. Is that correct?' Skroop asks, a hint of a smile crawling across his sickly lips. He looks like the cat that got the cream. And I am the cream.

'Is it or is it not true,' he snarls, 'that the three of you infected the entire school with head lice in a feeble attempt to avoid the upcoming examinations?'

'What does "feeble" mean?' Jack asks.

'ENOUGH! Not only will you be present for next week's exams, but you will handwash every hat in the school. And –' he raises his voice so that everybody can hear '– you will all spend Saturday at school in the hall at a boot camp in preparation for the national standardised tests, under *my* supervision, to make up for the disruption of the past few days.'

Kids gasp and call out 'Nooooo!', but Skroop doesn't mind at all. He's enjoying it. Jonah Flem says, 'But I've got soccer!' Miss Norrish shakes her head, disappointed. Jack and I have really done it this time.

'And *if* this school does below par in the exams, you three will have a one-hour after-school detention every day for the remainder of the year. Do you understand?' he asks.

'Yes, Mr Skroop.'

'Now, as a show of unity with the rest of your schoolmates, I would like you to rub heads with the new boy.'

I look at Skroop, not believing what I have heard. This is not the way deputy principals are supposed to behave. But Mr Skroop is not your everyday deputy principal. He is a deeply disturbed individual.

'Go on,' he says. 'Chop-chop.'

'But . . .' I look around to some of the teachers, waiting for them to step in. But none of them does. A few parents have gathered at the side and rear doors. They watch on – teachers, kids, parents – all hungry to see our public downfall.

I look at Lewis's hair. It is alive with nits, like a tree full of small birds. I can't do this. I'm going to run. It's the only way.

But, before I do, Skroop grabs Jack's head and my head and smooshes them into Lewis's hair. My ear is pressed against Lewis's ear. I swear I can feel those filthy little minibeasts scurrying onto my scalp. The kids erupt in applause and I realise, at that moment, that humans are sick.

Skroop releases his grip and Jack and I spring away from Lewis. Everyone watches on, silent once more.

I feel a slight tingling, then a definite itch at the back of my head. But I refuse to scratch.

I won't give them the satisfaction.

Now it's really itchy on top. And the sides. And my eyes start to water. The whole world is watching me and my head is ready to explode. I can't take it anymore. I scratch like mad and the crowd goes crazy, like their team just scored.

'Dis-*missed*!' Skroop announces. 'Have an enjoyable day!'

I have been inhabited.

What Would You Rather Do?

Jack and I were bored on the bus so we had a game of 'What Would You Rather Do?'. Here are some of our best . . .

What would you rather do . . .?

- Take a bath filled with red-back spiders or take a shower with 17 red-bellied black snakes?

- Brush a hungry tiger's teeth or fight a rhinoceros with a toothbrush?

- Kiss a girl on the lips or have a llama lick your tongue?

- Have a thick beard that covers your entire face for the rest of your life or have Dalmatian spots all over your body?

- Have your whole body covered in bees or eat a live-bee sandwich?

a live bEE sandwich

- Become a werewolf or a vampire?

- Eat 73 pieces of Vegemite on toast in one sitting or leap from a five-storey building into a giant bowl of cornflakes and milk?

the cereal's too fAr doWN dude!

- Have ten large dogs sneeze on your face or be chased by a vicious German shepherd?

- Have $100,000 in the bank and no friends or $0 in the bank and lots of friends?

- Get fired from a cannon or have a cannonball fired at you?

- Have the superpower where you can turn anything you like into a banana or the superpower where you eat a banana and you turn into a chimpanzee?

- Eat a handful of sleep from a dog's eye or a handful of wax from a cat's ear?

- Have $100 in cash or $500 worth of cheese sticks?

Despicable Her

'Hi, Tom-Tom,' Tanya says, walking into the kitchen. My sister. Evil genius. Four years older than me, hair in a ponytail, grin on her face. I glare at her from the dining table and slurp milk and cornflakes off my spoon.

'What are you doing today?' she asks, grabbing a can of Coke out of the fridge and popping the top with her teeth.

I move the giant cornflakes box across the dining table so I can't see her. I suddenly become really interested in the nutritional information. *0.1 grams of fat in each 30-gram serving.*

'I was thinking we should call a truce,' Tanya says, coming over to the table.

23.1 grams of carbohydrate. Thiamin. Riboflavin. Niacin.

Tanya holds out her hand. 'I'm sorry, okay?'

I look around the box and stare at the hand. Nails freshly painted with black nail polish. Thumb poking through a hole in the shredded cuff of her jumper. I check to see if there's a trick buzzer or anything in her hand. I look up at her. She looks like she's being honest, which is creepy because it's school holidays and Tanya and I have been at war for five solid weeks. We're like arch-enemy super-villains.

First day of the holidays she slopped bright orange fake tan onto my face while I was sleeping. My new nickname is 'Pumpkin-head'.

So I mixed a bunch of dead flies into the

box of Coco Pops, her favourite cereal. But then I forgot about it and ate a bowl myself the next morning.

After eating the flies I was so angry with her that I planted a pack of Tic Tacs on the kitchen table. I mixed in six of my baby teeth that were hidden in Mum's 'special things' box on top of her wardrobe. Tanya swallowed two of my teeth, which was cool. Except that I immediately thought about where they might exit her body, an image that will be with me till the day I die.

When she found out, she threw a copy of *The Complete Works of William Shakespeare* at me and it hit me in the face, breaking my nose. I'm still wearing giant, crisscross, heavy-duty bandaids on my snout. Who knew that

Shakespeare's plays were so heavy?

That was week one of the holidays. Things have gone downhill since then. Now I live in fear. Every step I take, everything I eat, every time I sit down, I'm on guard.

The Worst School Holidays Ever! A Memoir volume XIII

'I feel bad about your nose,' Tanya says. 'And Mum's going to lose it again if we keep fighting, and then she'll ground us. I need to go out on the weekend, so can we just be friends?'

I look at her hand again. 'What if you're tricking me?'

'I'm not. Seriously. I know I've been horrible but it's not because of you. It's other things that I'm annoyed about. Sorry for taking it out on you.'

I feel my hand slowly moving towards hers. *Stop*, I think. But I can't help it. I like it when she's nice to me. It only happens once a year for about four minutes but it still makes me feel good. Maybe this is my four minutes. Maybe I should get a photo of the two of us or something?

'Cool,' Tanya says, shaking my hand.

I move the cornflakes box out of the way and she sits down and puts her feet up on the dining table. She sucks the froth off the top of her can.

'Oh, I had an idea,' she says.

'Yeah? What?' I kind of hope she wants to play Scrabble. About two years ago we had a game in her room, but I was so excited that she was being nice to me I dropped my guard, lost muscle control and accidentally cut a stinker. She threw me out. That was the last time I saw the inside of her room.

'I want you to do all of my jobs for the next week or I'll tell Mum you stole that bubble gum from Papa Bear's.'

Papa Bear's is the shop on the corner of our street.

'What?' I ask.

'I said, either you do all of my jobs for the next week or I'll tell Mum you stole that bubble gum from Papa Bear's.'

look into the eyes of one of the GREAT evil minds of our time – MY sister!

'But I didn't steal any bubble gum from Papa Bear's.'

Tanya winks at me. 'Mum doesn't know that, Pumpkin-head.'

I sit there thinking about this, trying to understand the inner workings of one of the great evil minds of our time. 'But you just said you wanted to be friends. And how would you prove that I stole something that I didn't steal?'

'As if I would *ever* want to be friends with you. I've hidden some gum in your room,' she explains. 'Grape Hubba Bubba with two pieces missing. When Mum gets out of the shower I'll tell her that you stole some bubble gum and, when you deny it, I'll just tell her where you hid it. Simple.'

I look at her sitting opposite me at the table, still trying to get my head around her scheme.

'So?' she says, letting sticky Coke saliva

drip down past her chin before sucking it back up again. 'Do we have a deal? All my jobs for the next week?'

'And what do I get?' I ask.

'You get to keep your secret.'

'I don't have a secret.'

'Yes, you do. You stole a packet of grape Hubba Bubba, hid it in your room, confided in me and I'm doing what any responsible big sister would do. I'm telling Mum so that she can deal with the matter like an honest, upstanding citizen, by taking you to Papa Bear's to admit to the owner what you stole.'

'But I didn't steal anything,' I tell her.

Mum walks in with a towel on her head. She flicks on the kettle. 'Morning.'

'Hi, Mum,' Tanya says, cheerful. 'Tom's been telling me about something he did, and I really think it's best you know.'

My eyes widen.

'If this is you two dobbing on one another

again, I don't want to hear it,' Mum says.

'It's kind of big, Mum. I think you would want to know.'

Mum turns to us. 'What have you done this time, Tom?'

I look at her. I look at Tanya. 'Nothing,' I say. I stand, walk to the dishwasher and start emptying it.

'That's Tanya's job,' Mum says.

'I know. But I don't mind doing it.'

Mum looks at me and then at Tanya. 'Whatever it is, leave me out of it.' She heads down the hall.

'Good boy, Tom-Tom,' Tanya says, crushing her can and tossing it in the middle of the kitchen floor. Brown, sticky liquid seeps out onto the floorboards. 'Clean that up for me, will you?' She walks across to me, leans right into my face and unleashes the loudest, most violent burp I have ever witnessed. She blows a mixture of Coke stink and morning breath right up my nose.

'Tom, don't be disgusting!' Mum calls.

'Sorry,' I yell back. I ball both fists,
scrunch my toes and bite down on my teeth
so hard I'm in danger of bursting an internal
organ.

Tanya laughs at my stiff-as-a-board body.
'Good boy, Tombles.'

Mum is at work all week and I spend the next
five days searching for the bubble gum and
doing *everything* for Tanya:

- Making snacks
- Ironing clothes
- Polishing shoes
- Making coffee
- Vacuuming the house
- Mopping
- Tidying
- Washing windows

- De-moulding the shower
- Cleaning the toilet

I have blisters, and I do such a good job that Mum gives Tanya extra pocket money for all the great work she's doing.

'You should take a leaf out of Tanya's book,' Mum tells me, 'rather than sitting around staring at screens all the time.'

I desperately want to tell her about Tanya's evil plan – I don't want Mum to think I'm a thief as well as being lazy and rude – but I can't work out how to do it.

On Saturday night I spend two hours turning my room upside down one final time, searching for the bubble gum. I dream of finding it, eating the whole packet and blowing the world's biggest bubble. In this dream, I put Tanya inside it and watch her float away into the sky, never to be seen again.

I look inside the trapdoor under the rug in

the middle of my bedroom floor. I sift through my Lego. I take every book off my shelf to see if she has carved a hiding space within the pages. I tip out my clothes from the drawers and check every pocket. I look under my bed and in the hole in my mattress. I search on top of my wardrobe, in the pebbles in my fish tank. I even get the ladder and look inside the manhole in the ceiling. I search every square millimetre of my room and I find nothing.

Mum comes in to say goodnight, sees how messy my room is and tells me off.

'But Tanya —'

'Don't "But Tanya" me. I'm talking about you, Thomas. Tanya's doing a fantastic job keeping the place tidy while I've been at work, trying to keep a roof over your head and food on your plate.'

'Yes, Mum. Sorry, Mum.'

'Goodnight.'

' 'night, Mum.'

I clean up my room and go to bed.

It's Sunday afternoon, the final day of my sentence. I'm actually happy to be going back to school tomorrow. Mum will be back from the supermarket any minute. It's Tanya's turn to cook, so I'm making hamburgers. I'm just putting cheese on the burgers when Tanya comes into the kitchen and dumps her netball stuff on the floor.

'Hamburgers? Couldn't you think of something better than that?'

'Sorry, master,' I say.

'You've got more cheese than me,' she says, pulling up a stool at the kitchen bench.

'Yes, master.' I slap another piece of cheese onto her burger, then throw the tomato on.

'I hate tomato. Don't give me tomato,' she says.

I want to throw the tomato at her. Instead, I calmly go to take it off her burger. 'Yes, master.'

'Don't use your fingers. Use tongs, you filthy animal,' she snipes.

I remove the tomato with tongs and place the burger patties on the buns. I squeeze sauce on.

'I want barbecue sauce, not tomato,' she says.

I pick the patty off her burger and I throw it at her face.

She ducks and it whizzes over her head, hitting the kitchen window. It slides down the glass, leaving a long, saucy trail.

She laughs, grabs my burger patty and throws it. It is flying towards me like a small beef frisbee. I know I can dodge it. I just need to trust my cat-like reflexes. I shift my head to the right and –

Schlap. It lands on my cheek, spraying sauce into my left eye.

The sound of a key in the front door.

'Hi guys, I'm ho-ome,' Mum calls.

'That's IT!' I scream at Tanya. 'I'm telling Mum.'

I charge out of the kitchen and down the hall.

'Mum, Tanya just threw a burger patty in my face, and you know what she's been doing for the past week?'

'Tom, the last thing I want to hear is you dobbing on Tanya the second I get in the door.'

Mum struggles down the hall past me with a bunch of shopping bags.

'But –'

'No more!'

She's serious, but I don't care. I'm a man possessed. I have been humiliated, shamed and made to work like a dog all week – and I'm not going to take it anymore.

I follow her into the kitchen.

'Tanya blackmailed me into doing jobs for her all week by saying she was going to tell you that I stole a packet of grape Hubba Bubba from the shop which is stupid because I don't even like grape Hubba Bubba and she said she hid a pack of it in my room and if I didn't do all her jobs she'd tell you I stole it and then show you where I hid it but I didn't hide it in the first place and *I'm* the one who cleaned the toilet and washed the windows and made dinner every night while Tanya did nothing and then she threw a hamburger patty at me!'

Mum drops the bags on the kitchen floor and rubs her eyes and face. She takes the milk and yoghurt out of a shopping bag and says, 'Tanya?'

'Well . . .' Tanya says, enjoying the moment. 'I don't even know what a grape Hubba Bubba is, and –'

'YOU!' I scream, launching myself at her.

Mum holds me back. 'Tom!'

'She's lying!'

'Settle down, Tom,' Mum says.

I pull back. My face tingles with rage.

'And in terms of the burger . . .' Tanya continues. 'He threw a burger at me first, and he didn't even clean it up. Look!' She points to the kitchen window where a slick trail of tomato sauce leads to a broken beef burger pattie on the windowsill.

'Tom, that's disgusting,' Mum says.

'If I stole bubble gum, show Mum where it is!' I stab the words at Tanya.

Tanya looks confused. 'Why would I think you stole bubble gum?' she says. 'I don't think you're a thief. I mean, you probably are, but that's your business. Mum, do you want me to make something else for dinner?'

'Yes thanks, that'd be lovely,' Mum says. 'There's a nice pumpkin there for soup.'

'Great!' Tanya kisses Mum on the cheek and smiles at me.

'Tom, go to your room,' Mum says.

'No!'

'Tom. Room. Now.'

I shake my head. 'No.'

'Okay, how about this? For being rude, you can do all of Tanya's jobs for the next week. Now, go!'

I scream in fury and frustration, turn and stomp to my room.

It has, officially, been the worst. School. Holidays. In the world. Ever.

A week later I'm at Papa Bear's buying bread for Mum and I have a brainwave. I figure I'll buy some gum and hide it in Tanya's room. I ask the guy at the counter for a pack of grape Hubba Bubba.

'Sorry, we don't sell it,' he says. 'Never have.'

Take Out Your Brain

well, I wasn't expecting that!

I've decided to have my brain removed. I think it's for the best. I've made a list of the pros and cons and I'm going to take the plunge. Here are my top ten reasons for having my brain removed and why you should think about losing yours, too.

1. Mum's always saying, 'Use your brain,' but if I didn't have one she probably wouldn't say it anymore. It would be kind of insensitive.

2. When Mr Skroop asks for my homework I could say, 'I'm sorry, I don't have a brain.' Skroop would probably reply with something like, 'Don't be smart,' and I could honestly say, 'I'm not.'

3. I will never have to wear a bike helmet again because there will be nothing to protect.

4. I will become the centre of attention at parties, doing a trick where I hold a candle up to my left ear and have someone blow in my right ear and put the candle out.

5. The average weight of the human brain at age 12 is 1.4 kilograms and here I am, like an idiot, carting all that extra weight around. It'll be the ultimate diet: 'Lose a kilo overnight!'

6. With all that empty space I'll be able to shove Tic Tacs in my ears and use my head as a maraca.

7. I won't have to eat tinned tuna sandwiches anymore. (They taste like cat food and make my schoolbag stink.) Mum forces me to eat them by saying that fish is good brain food, but if I didn't have a brain there would be no point. Nothing to feed.

8. If there is ever a zombie attack on Kings Bay I won't have to worry about a zombie eating my brain. In fact, I might keep my brain in a jar and use it as bait to lure a zombie to my house, then catch it and keep it as a pet. (Which is totally allowed under the United Nations Universal Declaration of Zombie Rights.)

9. With all that extra space in my skull I'll install a hard drive and download music and games. I'll play them all day in my head, and if Mum asks me to do something for her I'll say, 'An error has occurred. Shutting down. Please try again later.'

10. Life will be a total no-brainer.

Like a long, abandoned building.

Stella Holling: Sugar Rush

I think I must have done something wrong in a previous life, and payback is standing on my front doorstep.

'To-om!' she sings. 'Open u-up!'

I am in my lounge room, peering through a crack at the edge of the curtain. The TV mutters in the background. Stella Holling is on the veranda holding a large white box. She is freckled, skinny and short, with a chocolate-smothered mouth. She is wearing pink-and-white bunny ears on her head. I never thought she'd come here again. A man should feel safe in his own home.

'I know you're in there,' she says. 'Kissy, kiss-y!'

Stella Holling has been in love with me since second grade. One time, not too long ago, she tricked me into kissing her on the lips in front of about 50 high-school boys. It was the

There is something not quite right about Stella Holling, but I can't put my finger on it.

darkest day of my life. I still scrub my lips with soap every night but it doesn't wash away the pain.

At least, that time, we were in the playground. There were witnesses. Today, I'm home alone. Mum and my sister Tanya are out shopping. They'll be gone for hours.

I eke the curtain open a little more.

The chocolate smeared around Stella's mouth scares me, it really does. It's Easter Monday and I'll bet you 50 bucks she's been stuffing her gob with cheap chocolate for two days straight. And you know what the main ingredient in cheap chocolate is?

Sugar.

Stella goes cuckoo when she eats sugar. I once saw her scale the school flagpole after a handful of M&M's. Mr Barnes, the maintenance guy, had to climb the 13-metre extension ladder to save her.

I've been dodging Stella's phone calls for weeks. Every afternoon she rings me ten, 12, sometimes 20 times. Usually she doesn't say anything, but I know that wheezy breathing when her throat is thick with chocolate.

And it's been getting worse. On Thursday I ignored ten calls, then I picked up and screamed, 'Whaddya want, you creepy freak?' But it wasn't Stella. It was Mum. And she was really angry because I hadn't been answering the phone. I told her I'd been in the bath and she said, 'You haven't willingly taken a bath in your life, Tom Weekly.'

There's no way I could say that I didn't answer the phone because of Stella. I did that once and Mum rang Stella's mum, and they decided we should all get together to discuss the situation. She invited them over on a Saturday afternoon. The mums ate biscuits and drank tea and had the greatest time of their lives, while I was left to entertain Stella and show her around the house. She tried to kiss me on the cheek the second we were out of our mothers' sight and I screamed. Mum said, 'Stop being a baby, Tom.'

Me! A baby! I'm one of the toughest guys I know.

After Stella and her mother left, Mum said, 'Now that wasn't so bad, was it? Little Stella's not too scary for you, is she?' And she made me feel like I actually *was* a baby, which I'm not.

I know one thing for sure: Stella Holling is never setting foot inside this house again.

She pounds on the front door. 'Let me in, Tom. Please. I just want to give you your Easter present.'

She's staring right at me now. She knows I'm watching her from behind the curtain. She opens up the big white box. She bats her eyelashes, which makes me shiver. She reaches into the box and pulls out the largest Easter rabbit I've ever seen. It's the one from the window of the French patisserie on Jonson Street. It is smooth and wrapped in gold foil with a bright red ribbon around its neck, and the second I see it I know that I must have it. I have not eaten a single sliver of chocolate this Easter. Mum decided to give our Easter egg money to charity, so I went hungry and a kid in some faraway land got a rooster and a set of pencils. I know I should feel happy for him, but it's hard.

'Can I come in now?' Stella asks.

I move away from the window. I need time to think.

I want the rabbit but I cannot kiss Stella Holling. Not again. The question is, how do I get the rabbit without the kiss?

I go to the front door.

'Stella?' I call out.

'Yessy?' she says.

'You can leave the rabbit on the doorstep. Thank you for coming over . . . Happy Easter.'

I wait.

I listen.

I pray.

She giggles. 'You don't think I'm going to just leave this big, bootiful, expensive wabbit without seeing you in the flesh, do you?'

'Um . . . maybe?'

She giggles again. 'You're so silly, Tom. That's why I love you.'

'I would prefer that you didn't say that, Stella.'

'Why?'

'You know that I love Sasha,' I tell her for the millionth time.

'No, you don't. You just think you do.'

'Pretty sure I do.'

'Oh, Tom. You don't know what love is,' she says. 'You're just a boy. When we get married –'

'We're *not* getting married, Stella. For the last time, we are *not* getting married.'

'Not now, Mr Silly,' she says. 'It's not even *legal* to get married at our age. But when we're old enough . . . I've planned the whole thing. We're going to have –'

'ARE YOU GOING TO GIVE ME THE RABBIT OR NOT?' I shout.

Awkward pause.

'I will if you show some manners and don't act like a greedy, ungrateful little *piggy*.'

This is going to be more difficult than I thought.

'Just drop the rabbit on the doorstep and take three large steps back,' I say. 'Then I'll –'

'You drop the attitude and wash your mouth out with soap and water!' she snips. 'I'm getting the feeling you don't want to see me, Tom, which upsets me.'

'Don't get weird, Stella. It's just –'

I hear footsteps moving across the veranda.

'You still there?' I call.

Nothing.

'Stella?'

Silence.

I go to the window and peek out.

A breeze picks up, making Mum's hanging pot plants swing from side to side. The veranda's empty. She's gone.

The gate squeals at the side of the house.

The back door is open. I run, sliding across the floorboards and into the kitchen in my socks. Stella appears in the doorway and I slam the door shut, sliding the deadbolt across.

The next second Stella jams her head and an arm through the cat door. 'I love you, Tommy. Meowww!' She licks her paw and laughs her head off, then tries to scratch me.

I kneel down and push her shoulders, but she pushes back. I shove and she shoves back.

'Da putty tat's coming for you, Tommy,' she says. 'Meowww!'

She scratches me
and my cheek squeals
with pain, so I shove
even harder and
wrestle her out of the
cat door, then latch
it.

Stella goes
straight for the
window over the
sink. She rests the
chocolate bunny on

This is wHat I really
waNt to do wHen
stella Holling pokes
her HEAD through our
cat door.

the wheelie bin and hoists herself up to the
ledge. I slam the window down. She screams.
Her fingers are trapped in the gap beneath
the frame. I lift it a little and she pulls out
her fingers, holding them up – red, gnarled,
witch-like. Her freckles grow a darker shade
of brown.

'YOU!' she shouts, pointing a twisted
finger at me. She picks up the bunny and rips

off its ears, jamming them into her mouth, foil and all, and starts munching. Even through the closed window I can hear the metal scraping against her teeth. Then she turns and runs.

'Stella? Stella!'

I head out of the kitchen and down the hall. I check that the windows are locked in Tanya's room, my room, Mum's room. But I know it's not enough. Stella will stop at nothing to kiss me. She's only human. She probably has blueprints of the house. She's probably inside already. This thought freaks me.

I hear a ringing noise, but it's not the phone. I sneak back up the hall and into the lounge room. I stare at Mum's desk next to the fireplace. Her laptop is ringing. Nan is the only person we video call. Maybe she'll save me. I grab the mouse and click 'Answer Call'.

'Nan!' I say, but you know whose head pops up?

'Kissy, kiss-y,' Stella says, rolling her terrible eyes, gnashing her terrible, chocolate-coated teeth and wiggling her pink-and-white bunny ears. Her eyes spin. She has an earless rabbit under her arm. I don't recognise the dead, brown bushes behind her.

'Where are you?' I ask.

'Wouldn't you like to know?'

'How did you get my mum's username?'

She laughs like I've told the world's funniest joke. Then she snarls, 'Kiss me or the bunny gets it.'

I stare into the frightened rabbit's gold-foil eyes and I know that I must save it. That rabbit wants *me* to eat it, not Stella. My stomach groans with a deep chocolate hunger.

'My mum's gonna be home any minute,' I say.

'No, she's not. You're lying to me, Tom.' She holds up the rabbit.

'No, I'm not!'

'Stella Wella doesn't like her husband lying to her.'

'I'm not your –'

Stella snaps off the rabbit's head and bites off its nose.

'Hey!' I scream.

She ends the call.

Seconds later, the lights go out.

The TV and computer screens snap to black.

The fridge rattles to an eerie silence.

There's a scraping sound on the kitchen window.

Then a thump on the wall.

And a knock at the back door.

The lights flicker back on and then fall to black again. Terror rises in my chest and I feel the wax in my ears go all hot and runny.

There's a loud *bang* from the bathroom and I run down the hall. I put my ear to the door; I know she's in there. I can picture her creeping through the window. I have to stop her. It'll be difficult because when Stella eats sugar she displays superhuman strength.

Without another second's thought and with no concern for my own personal safety, I fling the door wide and strike a karate pose. 'Hi-YA!' I knew my yellow belt would come in handy sometime.

The room is empty. No Stella. No rabbit.

I check behind the door. I flick the shower curtain open. No one.

I hear a loud, insistent knock on the front door of the house. A pounding, like she's going at it with a jackhammer, trying to knock it down. I've had enough. I can't live like this, like an animal, cowering inside my own home at Easter time. I need to confront that freaky, freckle-faced stalker.

I go to my bedroom, peel back the rug, open my trapdoor and dig around to find my monster mask. It has wrinkled green skin with lumps of pus and sores all over it and a shock of wild, white hair. I'll scare the life out of her, she'll drop the rabbit, I'll grab it – or what's left of it – and in two minutes' time I'll be sitting on the couch with my friend the bunny rabbit.

I pull the mask on, close the trapdoor, roll the rug back into place and creep up the hall towards the front door. It's hard to see through the eyeholes and I bump into the hall table. Stella's pounding suddenly stops. There's a muffled flop and the house is silent.

My heart somersaults in my chest. I stand behind the front door and take the deadbolt knob between my fingers. I'm ready for anything. I breathe steadily and, in one quick motion, I rip the door open. 'RAAAAAAAAAAAAAAAAAARGH!'

The monster mask twists and I can't see out of the eyeholes, and when I straighten the mask I can't see Stella. She's gone.

Maybe she snuck into the house?

I tear the mask off . . . and guess who I find lying there on the veranda, flat out on her back?

'Stella?'

I prod her with my foot.

'Stella, get up. I know you're faking.' She doesn't move. 'I'm not that stupid, Stella.'

I go around to her left side and kneel down to check if she's breathing, but she doesn't seem to be. She really is very good at this. I feel a pang of nervousness. Maybe I scared her to death?

'Stella, you'd better not be tricking me. If you're faking and you're not dead, I'm going to be so annoyed with you.'

But it doesn't seem like she is faking. It feels like the real thing. I place two fingers on her neck to check her pulse. She's warm but I can't feel any beating. This frightens me because I know what people have to do in this situation. I practised it in Health class on a plastic dummy.

Mouth-to-mouth resuscitation.

Stella has so much brown goo on her face, it's mental. I can't put my lips on that. I try to wipe the chocolate off but it's too sticky. I can't even remember what I'm supposed to do. Do you breathe first then pump down on the chest, or is it chest then breathe? Stella looks pretty pale, though, so I figure I need to do something.

I lean down towards her. I look at her face close-up. I try to pretend that I am my best

friend Jack and that Jack is the one giving Stella mouth-to-mouth resuscitation, which makes me feel slightly better.

I check one more time to see if she's breathing but she's not, so I squeeze my eyes closed, press my lips against hers and blow.

Stella jerks forward and her face jams hard against mine, nearly knocking out my front teeth. My first thought is that I must have done something right because she's responding. But then my worst fears are confirmed. Stella's arms lock around my neck and I'm stuck. I try to struggle out of her hold, but she's got me and my mouth is smooshed up to hers. It's hideous. I am kissing Stella Holling through a mask of chocolate sludge and I want to bite off my own lips.

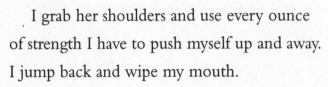

I grab her shoulders and use every ounce of strength I have to push myself up and away. I jump back and wipe my mouth.

65

She sits up, grinning like a mad person, bunny ears all crooked.

'That was *revolting*. I *knew* you were faking. Why would you do that?' I ask.

She gazes up at me, lovingly, like we've just exchanged wedding vows, like I've just kissed the bride.

'Gimme my rabbit,' I demand, holding out my hand.

'Can't,' she says.

'What do you mean "can't"? Yes, you can. You got your kiss. Now fess up the bunny.'

'In here,' she says, pointing to her belly and laughing. 'Yum, yum, yum! Happy Easter, Tommy!'

Nine Reasons Why Sloppy Food Should Be Banned

So, I went to my Nan's last night and she served a very sloppy, rank-smelling beef and vegetable curry for dinner. I think it may have been out of a can. I didn't have the heart to tell her that I'm allergic to sloppy food so I ate it. Then, to heal myself, I went home and wrote this list of reasons why sloppy food should be banned.

1. Sloppy food is for babies and old people, both of whom scare me with their gummy smiles and nappies.

2. Sloppy food usually has at least one hair of unknown origin in it.

3. I like snappy words like 'crisp' and 'pop' and 'crackle' and 'sharp'. 'Sloppy' is not a snappy word. It's more like 'ooze' and 'squelch' and 'squidgy' and 'gloop'.

4. When I was five I found Nan's false teeth in my potato and leek soup. Soup should not smile at you.

I trust your slop is to your liking sir?

5. The word 'sloppy' makes me think of sloppy joes – the shapeless, itchy green sacks they make us wear to school in winter.

6. Sloppy food reminds me of a horror movie I once saw where creamed corn squished out of a guy's belly button. Any food a filmmaker can use as a special effect for human gizzards should not be eaten.

7. Underpaid kitchen hands and angry waiters can spit or wee in sloppy food and stir it in without you ever knowing.

8. Soup is sloppy. Soup is a very bad food. Especially when it contains any of the three most repulsive substances known to humankind: pumpkin, eggplant and zucchini.

9. Sloppy food does not solidify as it travels through your body. Sloppy in. Sloppy out.

Mad Cat

My mum bought a cat. He's ginger.
His name is Gordon. And he's the
weirdest cat in the world. I know that
everyone says their cat is weird but
Gordon is YouTube weird. He makes
other bizarro cats seem normal. And
he's kind of creepy, too. Here are just
a few reasons why Gordon Weekly is
the world's freakiest cat:

- Last night, in the darkness of my
  bedroom, he smiled and spoke to me.
  Not in a good way.

- My mum has taught him to use a human toilet. There is nothing more frightening than sitting down on the toilet in the middle of the night and realising you've sat on a cat.

- His favourite place to sleep is on my face.

- He has a pocket on his front right side where he keeps miniature throwing knives and a short length of rope.

- Last week, I caught him smoking a cigar late at night on the back veranda.

- He uses one paw to stop the bell around his neck from ringing and then walks on three legs so that he can sneak up on birds and eat them.

- If you tease him and say the words 'I tawt I taw a puddy tat,' he scratches you. I used to think it was funny until I had to have the eye operation.

- He licks his own bottom.

- Then he licks me.

- He sometimes sleeps in my clothes drawers and, last night, he vomited inside my favourite undies. But I didn't have a spare pair so I had to wear them to school. Luckily Tuesday's canteen special is fish burgers, which helped hide the smell.

- His favourite food is M&M's (chocolate is supposed to be poison for cats, but not for Gordon) and he won't drink milk – only pineapple juice.

- He likes to leave little presents for me. On his second day in the house, he dragged home a chihuahua and dumped it on the front doorstep.

- He sneaks out late at night and, once, I followed him to an alley off the main street where there were a dozen other mean-looking cats betting on a mouse race.

- He's building what looks like a bazooka out of empty cat-food tins over behind Bando's kennel. I think he's planning to use it on me. This means war.

CDS

Jack's dad has a terrible disease. It's something that fathers have suffered from since the dawn of time: CDS. Cranky Dad Syndrome. Maybe your dad has it, too?

Mr D has been going to classes to deal with his CDS. A bunch of fathers meditate and watch videos of dolphins and wear beads around their necks to stop them exploding every time their kid does something wrong.

He's really made progress. He's been in a heaps better mood. But Jack misses the old Mr D. Cranky Dad Syndrome made life interesting, stirred things up a bit. It was like living in a wave pool at a theme park and now he's stuck in a duck pond with a father who's calm and polite but kind of boring.

So it's Saturday morning and Jack and I are on a mission to save Mr D, to reunite him with his inner Cranky Dad, to bring back CDS.

Mr D
trying not
to burst.

'Jack! Did you replace the remote control batteries with sausages?' Mr D says, coming into Jack's bedroom. He holds up the remote and a handful of mashed sausage meat.

'No, Dad,' Jack says innocently. He and I are playing Monopoly on the bed.

'Who else around here would do

something that stupid?' Mr D asks.

'Dunno,' Jack says.

Mr D growls. 'Are there any other batteries?'

'Dunno,' Jack says.

'Well, can we change the channel without the remote? It seems to be stuck on *Thomas the Tank Engine* at the moment.'

'Nope.'

'This is *ridiculous*!' Mr D raises his voice. It's World Cup time and he has his lucky Socceroos jersey on. He bought it when he was a teenager. His gut hangs out now and the sleeves are too short but he totally believes that wearing it gives Australia an edge.

Mr D has not yet realised that he only has half a moustache. Jack snuck into his bedroom at 6.15 am and shaved off the left side before he woke up.

'Are you *sure* you didn't do this to the remote, Jack?'

'Yes, Dad.'

'Because if you did . . .'

'I didn't, Daddy.' Jack grins at his Dad.

Mr D looks as though he wants to dissect Jack like a laboratory rat. But, instead, he starts to whistle. It's one of the techniques from his classes. He's whistling 'O Christmas Tree'. Or it could be 'Do You Know the Muffin Man?' I can't really tell. He's hasn't had that much practice yet. After ten seconds or so, Mr D speaks, in a calm, deliberate voice.

'Don't call me "Daddy". The game's on in 15 minutes. I'm going to the shop to get batteries.'

He heads up the dimly lit front hall and reaches to get his keys off the brass hook, but they're not there.

'Has anyone seen my keys?' he shouts.

'On the hook near the front door?' Jack calls from his room.

'If they were on the *hook*, why would I ask

you, my *little buddy*?' he calls back.

'Well, they'll be wherever you put them,' Jack says.

Mr D rubs his forehead.

'Three seconds till I have my old dad back,' Jack whispers. 'This was easier than I thought it'd be. Three . . .'

We peek through the crack near the hinges of Jack's door as Mr D searches his pockets.

'Two . . .' Jack whispers.

Mr D rifles through a drawer in the cabinet near the front door.

'One . . .'

He slams the drawer shut and closes his eyes. He fondles the beads hanging from his neck with his chunky, bricklayer's fingers. Jack and I poke our heads around the door, watching him carefully, waiting for him to erupt. Mr D opens his eyes and looks right at us.

'Jacko, have you seen my keys, mate?' he says calmly.

'No, Grandma,' Jack says. 'I haven't.'

I cover my eyes.

'Please, don't call me "Grandma". And are you sure you don't have the keys?' he asks.

'Yep. I'm sure . . . Grandma.'

Mr D has a good, long look at Jack. He takes a small bag of lavender – a stinky purple flower – out of his pocket and has a long, deep sniff, then he breathes out very slowly. 'Not to worry,' he says. 'I'll find them. Still got 14 minutes.' Mr D heads down the hallway, past us and into the lounge room.

'These classes are making him weird,' Jack says. 'He's no fun anymore.' He takes the keys out of his pocket, goes to the front door, reaches up and hangs them on the hook. 'Have you got the biscuits?'

'In my bag,' I tell him.

'Activate Phase Two.'

I grab my backpack and we sneak out the front door. It's raining outside, so we work quickly. I stack eight packets of Monte Carlo biscuits on the bonnet of Mr D's work ute. We open the packets, pull each biscuit apart and stick the two halves to the ute, using the cream as glue. We stick biscuits all over the doors, the roof, the windows, the bonnet. We can't stop laughing as we do it. But it's that nervous laugh when you know that something very, very bad is about to happen.

mr D's utE witH a bad case of THE Monte Carlos.

Six minutes later we're back inside, standing at the laundry door. Mr D is on his knees surrounded by mounds of stinking clothes, searching through the hamper.

'Eight minutes till game time,' Jack says.

Mr D looks up at us.

'Must be sooo frustrating, Dad. Where could they be?'

This kind of comment would, ordinarily, send Mr D into a frothing fit, but he just calmly piles clothes back into the hamper.

'Maybe the keys are in the ute?' Jack suggests.

Mr D looks at Jack, heads out of the laundry and walks down the hall. We follow him. As he goes out the front door he sees his keys hanging from the hook. He turns, slowly, to us.

'Is this your idea of a joke?' he asks.

'No, Granny,' Jack says, smiling.

'Did you have my keys all along?'

'No, Granny,' Jack says.

'*Don't* call me "Granny"!'

'I thought you just didn't want me calling you "Grandma"?'

'Do you think I'm some kind of *fool*?' he says, raising his voice.

Here he comes. I can almost smell the old Mr D now. I'm kind of glad the mission is over before he sees what we did to his ute. Maybe we can clean it up before he realises. Mr D wipes sweat from his forehead with the palm of his hand and whispers the word 'mango' to himself.

'Mango' is his emergency code word, to help snap him out of a fast-approaching CDS attack.

He takes a deep breath, closes his eyes for a moment, then smiles.

Jack can feel victory slipping through his fingers. He panics and says, 'Okay, I admit it. I did take your keys.'

Mr D repeats the word 'mango' under his breath seven or eight times. A deep crease appears in the space between his eyes. 'Okay . . . well . . . that's good of you to be honest, Jack. No harm done.'

Jack has had enough. 'No *harm* done?' He walks down the hall towards his dad. 'What do you mean, "no harm done"? You were on your hands and knees searching through my dirty undies on the laundry floor. You rummaged around the entire house. It's *five* minutes till game time, and you can't even change the channel. What's happened to you, Dad? Doesn't any of this make you even a *little* bit cranky?'

Mr D thinks about it for a moment, then

says, 'I'm a new man, Jacko. Nothing can break me.'

'It's the *semifinal*,' Jack says. 'Australia never gets into the finals. This is a once-in-a-lifetime opportunity.'

'Well, I better get going then. I'll be back before the starting whistle.' He grabs his keys and gets ready to leave.

'This is *mental*,' Jack says. 'What if I were to tell you that I put the sausages in the remote?'

Mr D stops in the doorway. He turns to Jack. He looks down at his hand where I can still see a fleck of sausage meat. He swallows hard. He strokes his left earlobe firmly three times. Then he smiles again. 'You and your practical jokes.' He ruffles Jack's hair. 'You'll be a comedian one day.' He heads out the door.

'Maybe he's cured,' I suggest.

'Just wait.'

'Jack!' Mr D calls.

'Yes, Dad,' Jack replies.

'Why is my ute covered in biscuits? And birds?'

We step out the front door. It's sprinkling outside. Mr D has stopped halfway down the front path. He is staring at his work ute which sits in the driveway. And it's true. Not only does the ute look like a five-year-old's birthday cake, but there are about 15 magpies on the car feasting on the Monte Carlos.

'Would you believe it if I said it was some of the neighbourhood kids?' Jack asks.

Mr D stands there in the rain, glaring at us. He walks up the front steps, towards us.

We back up into the house.

'I don't think it *was* the neighbourhood kids,' he says. 'I think it was *you*, Jack. You and your numbskull mate.'

'No way. Wasn't us.'

Mr D clenches and unclenches his fists, making his way slowly across the front deck.

His half-moustache makes him look lopsided and menacing. The rain pelts down harder now. I'm getting a little nervous, I really am. Mr D looks like he's about to strangle someone.

'This is it,' Jack whispers out of the side of his mouth.

'You two ...' he says, his shadow falling across us.

WHOA! How'd this hole get here?

Exploding Dad.

I wish I'd never got involved in this. I wish I'd never bought those biscuits. I wish Jack had never been born. Mr D looks as angry as I've ever seen him – a white-hot nuclear reactor of a man with a twitchy left eye. In a cartoon, he'd have steam billowing from his ears. It's a miracle of human biology that this much pressure and tension can build up inside one man. He starts to rock from foot to foot, mumbling 'mango,' sniffing his lavender, counting his beads and stroking his earlobe like he's about to rip it off – but none of it does any good. It's too late. The reactor is ready to blow and I can't take it anymore. I plunge my hand into Jack's pocket and pull out the two AA batteries he took from the remote.

'Here!' I scream, holding them up in front of Mr D's face.

He looks at the batteries, then at me and Jack, then back at the batteries.

'You idiot!' Jack spits.

Mr D lets go of his ear and pockets the lavender. His eye stops twitching. The reactor cools rapidly. Within seconds he looks almost like a regular human. He calmly takes the batteries from my hand.

'Thank you, Tom. I owe you one. Now,

you boys don't seem to be doing much. Would you mind going and cleaning those bickies and birds off the ute? Shouldn't take you long. You'll be finished by the time the game's over.'

'But I want to watch it!' Jack complains.

'Well, that's a bit of bad luck . . . Grandma.' Mr D pushes past us and heads inside.

Jack smacks me on the back of the head.

Cleaning up 320 biscuit halves is more difficult than you might think. First we have to battle the magpies. Twenty-five minutes, 13 swoops and a couple of flesh wounds later, we start working on the biscuits. They have gone soggy in the pouring rain and they squish between my fingers as I scrape them off the bonnet and chuck them into the wheelie bin.

Jack eats most of the biscuits he peels, licking the jammy cream off his fingertips and trying to dodge the ones with bird poo on them. I tell him he'll end up with bird flu but he doesn't seem to care.

Halfway through the job, out of nowhere, there's an animal roar from inside the house and the magpies – who have been snickering at us while we work – flee the gum tree overhanging the ute.

'Jack! Did you shave off half my moustache? JACK!'

25 Ways to Test Your Dad for Cranky Dad Syndrome

CDS – Cranky Dad Syndrome – is a serious disorder, not to be ignored. It results in more Australian children being grounded, banned from watching TV and forced to do jobs around the house than any other known illness.

Here are 25 CDS testing techniques suggested by kids in my playground. Do NOT try these at home.

1. Squeeze superglue onto his hand when he's sleeping and tickle his face with a feather so he glues his hand to his face. – *Auburn*

2. 'Accidentally' switch channels when a try is about to be scored in the football. – *Sage*

3. Put worms in spaghetti and serve it as breakfast in bed. – *Paco*

4. Paint his nails pink. – *Malack*

5. Put an impossible password on his laptop. – *Mariam*

6. Put your feet on the table and eat like a cow during dinner. – *Charlotte*

7. Make him watch a romantic comedy movie marathon. – *Jess*

8. Tell him you like your uncle better. – *Lucy*

9. Don't eat dinner and, when he says you can stay up all night till it's eaten, actually stay up all night. – *Ivy*

10. Place dog poo on the floor beside his bed in the middle of the night. – *Archie*

11. Hang his dirty undies around the house as ornaments when VIPs are coming for dinner. – *Sofia*

12. If you have a dog, follow it around on all fours and say 'bark' over and over again really loudly. – *Stacey*

13. Randomly pluck someone's hair out and scream 'DNA!' as loud as you can. – *Stacey*

14. In the grocery store, try to stick as many melons down your pants as possible, then start dancing. – *Stacey*

15. Destroy the house and then tell him, 'I love you, Daddy.' – *Stacey*

16. Say, 'I can't clean up my room because I'm doing a science experiment on the effect of excessive dust and mould on the human body.' – *James*

17. Spill coffee on his shirt before he goes to work. – *Jordan*

18. Set a slime trap for when he gets home from a hard day. – *Patrick*

19. Wake him up by slapping him with a maths book. – *Khyl*

20. Release three rats and a possum into the ceiling of your house. – *Nate*

21. Hide his undies. – *Kohl*

22. Change his favourite sauce to extremely hot wasabi. – *Khyl*

23. Speak in initials. Only say the first letter of every word. – *Kashalyn*

24. Let the chickens poo in his bed. – *Tia*

25. Give him laxatives (which make you need to use the toilet), then superglue shut all of the toilet seats in the house. – *Brody*

If you have any other ideas for diagnosing CDS, email me at: TheTomWeekly@gmail.com

The Great Escape

Pop finishes putting on his lipstick and takes a step back from the bathroom mirror.

'How do I look?' he asks.

'Well . . .' I say, trying to think of the nicest way to tell him that he is the ugliest man-dressed-as-a-woman I've ever seen. I glance down at his hairy feet, bursting from the black, thick-soled nurse's shoes. His light blue dress is crushed and crumpled. The badge reads 'Miriam Gooch – Head Nurse'. And his face? The smeared red lipstick, electric blue

eye shadow
and bright red
circles on his
cheeks make me
think 'demented
clown'.

'You look
great,' I say.
'Very convincing.' Although it's totally weird
seeing Pop not wearing yellow undies – that's
been his uniform for as far back as I can
remember. '*Now* can you tell me why you're
dressed as the head nurse?'

He looks over his shoulder at the
bathroom door, then back to me. His eyes are
wild and blue with a storm brewing behind
them. He snaps on the old radio that sits on
the vanity next to the cold tap. There's a
horse race on and he cranks up the volume.

'The place is bugged!' he says loudly.
'Can't be too careful.'

'Aren't they more likely to hear us if we're shouting?' I reach to turn the radio down but he slaps my hand away.

'I need you to help me,' he says, pulling me close.

'With what?'

He glances at the door again. 'I have a plan to break out of here.'

My eyes roll. Pop has told me this at least a thousand times over the past year since he's been in the nursing home. Once he tried to get me to hide a drill in a pavlova so that he could escape through the air-conditioning vent. Another time he attempted to hijack the minibus on an excursion to Tropical Fruit World. And the worst was when he made me sing 'Jingle Bells' at Christmas Eve karaoke while he snuck down the fire escape.

'I heard that, Cliff!' says a voice from outside the bathroom door. It sounds like Debbie, the unnaturally happy nurse.

'Told you the place is bugged!' Pop screams. 'How long'd it take 'em to send one of their operatives? Two seconds? Can't a man have some privacy without the enemy stickin' their big beaks into it?'

'We're not the enemy, Cliff,' Debbie calls sweetly.

'Ha!' he shouts. 'That's what the enemy always says.'

I snap off the radio.

'Stay here,' I whisper. I take a breath, unlock the bathroom door and slip out into Pop's room through the thinnest gap possible, closing the door behind me.

'Hello-o!' says Debbie, red-faced, straw-haired and jolly. 'What are you doing in there? Is Cliff coming out?'

'He's ... um ... trying to do a poo,' I tell her. It's the first thing that comes to me.

Debbie turns up her nose.

'I mean ... using the bathroom.'

'Were you helping him?' she asks.

I don't want to say 'yes'. I try to think of a good reason why I was in the bathroom while my pop was doing a number two, but I'm taking too long.

'Yes,' I say. 'I was helping him.'

'He's usually okay,' she says. 'Must be the haemorrhoids again. How about I leave you some cream and you can help him put it on when he's finished. It's quite straightforward. You just have to —'

'It's okay. I know how to do it.' There's no way I'm going to listen to a graphic description of how to apply haemorrhoid cream to my grandfather's bottom.

'Oh . . . okay,' she says. 'Just make sure he wipes properly.'

I taste a small amount of vomit in my throat as she fishes the cream out of her deep pocket and hands me the tube.

'Byeee,' she sings.

Haemorrhoid cream.

WHATEVER you do, Never look up 'haemorrhoid' in the dictionary.

'Seeeya,' I sing back.

Debbie leaves. I close the door. Pop emerges from the bathroom, adjusting the oranges he is using as breasts. 'Thanks, mate,' he says. 'Now, I'm going to try to walk right out the front door, but if anything goes wrong, I need you to whistle for reinforcement.'

'I'm not sure about this, Pop.'

'Bah! Don't be so negative. I've got to get out of this stinking hole. The food's disgraceful. I haven't tasted such slop since your grandmother mixed cat food into the meatloaf. I've got to swallow 140 tablets a day and have poisoned cream rubbed into my backside. Are you going to help me or what?'

Pop is really close to my face now. I can feel a couple of his wild eyebrow hairs tickling my forehead. I lean back a little. 'I guess,' I say.

A villainous grimace screams across his lipsticked mouth. 'Good boy. Now zip me up.'

He turns to the door and I see that the zip on his dress isn't done up at the back. Pop is busting right out of it. I can see a giant 'V' of hairy Pop back. I try doing it up but his fur gets caught in the zipper.

'Where did you even get this?' I ask.

'Stole it when the head nurse was having a shower 15 minutes ago. Now, remember, if anyone breaks my cover, whistle for backup.'

'But –'

'Foller me up the hall!' he says. 'You're my wingman.' He slips out the door and into the hallway. I poke my head out to find that hardly anyone's around. I figure it's a 50-metre walk up the long, straight corridor before he hits the revolving front door and he's free.

Pop strides towards the nurses' station, which is a room on the left, halfway up. I follow, sticking close to the wall. There's a nurse chatting to someone in the hall. I send out a prayer that she doesn't turn and see Pop hobbling along in the head nurse's shoes.

Pop is almost at the station when the nurse turns and walks towards him. Towards us. This is bad. Not only because my grandfather is dressed as a woman in a public place but because I don't know if this is an emergency, so I don't know whether to whistle for backup.

The nurse is walking with her head down,

reading something on a chart. As she passes, she glances up briefly and smiles.

I can't believe it. He seems to have convinced her that he's Head Nurse Gooch. This is impossible. She must be a frightening lady.

Just as the nurse reaches me, she turns back to Pop and says. 'Oh, Miriam. I meant to ask –' She stops mid-sentence. She sees what I see: Pop's gorilla back.

Pick THE real NursE.
(it's tricky I know,
but look closely).

She screams. Pop looks over his shoulder and starts hobbling up the hall again, double-time. Three nurses emerge from rooms at either side of the hallway: two men and a lady. Pop's outnumbered. They close in on him. I feel so sad. But then I remember my job. I jam my fingers into my mouth and give the loudest whistle I have ever given. This is definitely an emergency.

Eleven Kings Bay Nursing Home inmates – men and women aged 75 to 104 – spring from their rooms and fall into a V formation, surging up the corridor. It's a ready-made army. Reg Hopper, who used to own the toy shop, is up front in a motorised cart. He wears a pacemaker on his chest to keep his heart thumping. Behind him, five foot soldiers walk with canes, three are in wheelchairs, two are pushing oxygen tanks on stands.

They stagger and creak and wheeze their way up the hall, united by one thing: yellow

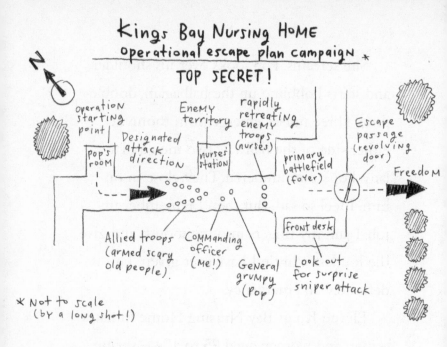

Kings Bay Nursing Home
operational escape plan campaign *
TOP SECRET!

N

operation starting point

Enemy territory

rapidly retreating enemy troops (nurses)

Escape passage (revolving door)

Pop's room

Designated attack direction

nurses' station

primary battlefield (foyer)

Freedom

Allied troops (armed scary old people).

Commanding officer (Me!)

General grumpy (Pop)

front desk

Look out for surprise sniper attack

* Not to scale (by a long shot!)

undies. They are all wearing yellow underpants just like Pop usually does. The ladies have their nighties tucked into them. The men wear the undies and nothing else. It's hideous. It's horrendous. I want to scratch my own eyes out. But it's strangely heartwarming and inspiring, too. They look ferocious, determined.

All are ready for combat.

Each member of Pop's army wields a

weapon of some kind. Betty Brown, who used to work at the post office, has a plate of disgusting nursing-home meatballs in her lap . . . and a slingshot. Mr Payne, an ex-policeman with ghost-white skin and a black eye patch, carries a bedpan that sloshes up around the edges. A lady at the back, solid as a tree, carries a quiver of sharpened walking sticks.

The three nurses at the station begin to retreat.

Pop starts moving forward again, and so do I. Pop's army is right behind me.

The three nurses look genuinely scared as they continue to back up the hall. One of them smashes the glass covering the emergency button on the wall and raises the alarm. *Bluuuuurp, bluuuuuurp, bluuuuuurp.*

'Go, Cliff!' someone shouts from behind me.

'We've got your back, Cliffy!'

'Send us a postcard from the other side!'

My body zings and thrings with electricity. Pop is going home. It feels important all of a sudden, like we're striking a blow for old people everywhere. We reach the large, bright entrance foyer at the front of the nursing home. There is a cheer from behind. The revolving door is ten metres away, just past the front desk, and the sweet smell of freedom is everywhere.

That's when a tall, skinny woman pops out from behind the desk. Her wet hair drips down her face. She is wrapped in a towel.

Pop stops. So do I.

Bluuuuurp, bluuuuurp, bluuuuurp. The alarm continues.

'I've been looking for that,' she shouts, eyeing Pop's dress.

I get the feeling that this might be the head nurse, Miriam Gooch.

'You're just jealous that I look better in it than you do, Gooch!' Pop snaps back.

'You are the ugliest man-dressed-as-a-woman I've ever seen, Weekly,' she sniggers as she moves in on Pop.

I couldn't have put it better myself.

'Get outta my way,' Pop demands. He attempts to storm past her but she cuts him off. He dodges the other way but she cuts him off there, too. She is youngish and strong and nimble, and she grabs the front of his dress. An orange slips out and rolls across the floor.

'Let him go,' I say.

She signals with a jerk of her head to a big, burly male nurse who grabs Pop's right arm.

'You leave me with no choice, Miriam,' Pop says. '*Open fire!*'

A meatball whizzes past my ear, spattering my cheek with tomato sauce before hitting Head Nurse Gooch in the neck. The contents of a bedpan decorate the back of the burly nurse's uniform and he releases his grip on Pop's arm. I duck just in time to be missed by a volley of sharpened walking sticks, hurled like spears.

Pop's troops are armed to the teeth with innovative weaponry like you've never seen before. There are balloons filled with hundreds of untaken pills that scatter on impact, turning the floor into a slippery skating rink. Plastic body parts are fired from a bandage-and-crutch catapult – an elbow, then a hand, and a prosthetic foot fly by, knocking the head nurse to the ground. Hankies rigid with snot are thrown like frisbees and false teeth are used as knuckledusters.

There's a loud bang from behind me and smoke fills the room, providing temporary cover for Pop to duck and weave his way through the battlefield. I follow closely behind. He makes it to the revolving door just as the smoke starts to clear.

I'm certain he's going to make it when the head nurse springs from the floor, still wearing just a towel, and grabs a tuft of fur on Pop's hairy back. He yelps. She spins him around to face his own troops and the battalion of shabby, beaten nurses.

Bluuuuurp, bluuuuurp.

a brief HISTORY of weapoNs of little destructioN

boiled Pterodactyl egg

medieval chocolate pudding sling

MEAt pie cannon

meatball SLING shot

'Will someone shut that darn thing off!'
she screams.

The alarm stops immediately.

The nursing home falls to near silence.
The only sound is the high-pitched squeal of a
dozen hearing-aid batteries dying.

'Now, Cliff,' says Head Nurse Gooch in a
creepy-calm voice, tightening her grip on his
back carpet. 'We're going to give you a little
something to help you calm down.'

'Over my dead body!' Pop shouts.

'If necessary,' Head Nurse mutters.

'And let go of my back hair,' Pop
demands. 'It pinches.'

'I can't let you go because I have a duty
of care,' she says. She flicks her head and
two of the nurses who were in the corridor
earlier move in on Pop – a stumpy man with
a greasy face and a lady with neat, black Lego
hair. The man clutches something in his
pocket.

'I just want to go home,' Pop says, his voice cracking. But the fight's gone out of him. He's tired. I turn to see Pop's army retreating. Reg Hopper leads them. Wheelchair tyres squeak and walking frames clack as they withdraw.

'We tried, Cliffy,' one of them calls.

'Thought we had 'em.'

'Never say die,' Betty whispers, and she winks at Pop before turning to follow the others down the hall.

'Just keep still,' Head Nurse says. 'This won't hurt a bit.'

The male nurse pulls the thing out of his pocket. It is a long, thin needle. The Lego-hair lady nurse holds Pop firmly by the arm. Head Nurse's eyes hunger to see the tip of the needle puncture Pop's paper-thin skin.

As the sharp point makes contact there's a loud 'Oi!' from Reg Hopper, who's suddenly right behind us – he's returned to the war front! Reg rams into the back of the greasy, needle-toting nurse's legs with his motorised cart. The nurse buckles to his knees.

'Hop on!' Reg says.

Pop goes to jump on behind Reg.

'Don't think so,' says Head Nurse. She and Lego Hair try to stop him.

But Reg Hopper has saved the best weapon till last. He stabs a button on a small device and a blue laser, the length of a sword, shoots from the end. It looks like he's hot-wired his pacemaker and turned it into some kind of lightsaber or tractor beam. With a *zzzzz* sound, Reg waves the beam at Head Nurse and she reels backwards. The stumpy, greasy little nurse holding the needle moves in. Reg captures the pointy weapon in his blue beam, flicks his wrist and the needle spins up into the air and comes down, jabbing into the nurse's cheek. The force of the impact squeezes the needle's contents into his face.

He squeals like a piglet, his eyes close and he stumbles backwards, his bottom landing in a large pot plant next to the front door. He's out cold.

Pop and I jump on the back of the cart, Pop gripping Reg's hips and me gripping Pop's.

Reg revs the engine and shouts, 'Hang on, boys. I've made a few modifications.'

Head Nurse blocks the front door so Reg lets out the brake, does a U-turn and we *shoom* across the foyer at hyper-speed. Reg charges through the debris from the battle, sloshing

HYPER - SPEED

through puddles from the bedpans, mashing meatballs and sending plastic body parts flying. We soar down the hall and nurses scatter. We scream around the corner into the communal TV room to find the other ten members of Pop's army. For some reason, they're not wearing their yellow undies anymore. They urge us on, making a tunnel of nude and nightied pensioners, jumping up and down, cheering, their bits bouncing all over the place. I shield my eyes from the horror as Reg squeals to a stop on the lino floor right in front of the window.

'Go, Cliff!' someone shouts.

'Be careful, old boy!'

Pop and I jump off the cart and look out the window.

The troops have gathered all their yellow undies and tied them into a rope, which is hanging from the window and down to the steeply sloping ground ten metres below.

Reg and Betty give Pop a boost up to the window frame as a cavalry of nurses arrives in the doorway. 'Grab him!' Head Nurse commands, and they push through the throng of inmates.

Pop kicks off his shoes, holds tight to the undie rope and leans out from the building. As a parting gift he pulls the other orange from his dress, hurls it at Head Nurse and drops out of view. I poke my head out to see Pop abseiling down the side of the building, pushing off the bricks with the world's crustiest feet. The oldies urge him on as Head Nurse goes to grab the yellow rope. Pop lands in the garden bed with a *whump*. Reg Hopper shoves Head Nurse out of the way and snips the rope, letting it fall to the ground.

'Yipeee!' Pop shouts, standing and dancing a little jig. He leaps from the garden and scurries across the grass.

'Take him down and bring him in!' Head

Nurse demands. A couple of offsiders run out the door and down the corridor to the front of the nursing home.

The oldies watch Pop, eyes glimmering, urging him on. It's as if each one of them is imagining themselves escaping, being as brave – or crazy – as my grandfather.

Pop limps and stumbles to the bush on the other side of the road that runs through the nursing home grounds. At the edge of the tree line he turns, bows and disappears into the shadows. The crowd roars around me. Betty and one of the old guys cry. Others look ten years younger and 30 years happier.

My pop is a hero. He's living everyone's dream. He's going home.

Well, he was.

He didn't quite make it home. He raced through the bush behind the nursing home, crossing a creek several times in an attempt to shake his scent. The nurses eventually picked him up at a 7-Eleven across the highway, with a handful of scratchies and a ginger beer. He was only gone 37 minutes but he reckons they were the best 37 minutes of his life.

Pop is a hero in the nursing home now. The residents are filled with hope again. They know it's possible. For one beautiful moment in time, one of them made it out. He loves being a celebrity, but when Nan visits she calls him a ninny and tells him he could have broken a hip.

Every Thursday afternoon at 4.00 pm, all the inmates gather in the dining room and Pop tells them the story of his escape. Every week the battle gets bigger and better and more ferocious. But the part they really like is when Pop tells them what the bush smelt like, the sound of the birds overhead, the taste of fresh air and the feeling of creek water running between his toes.

And, on special occasions, Pop steals a nurse's dress, puts on some lipstick and tells the story in full costume.

Best Slime Recipe

Ingredients

- Oats
- Plain flour
- Lime jelly crystals
- Green food colouring
- Water

Method

Mix ingredients in a bucket with a wooden spoon. Experiment with how much of each ingredient to add so you get your perfect slime consistency. Be careful not to use too much water.

Application

Slime has multiple uses. You could:

- have a slime fight in the backyard.

- play a board game or a sport with one of your parents. The winner gets to pour a bucket of slime on the loser's head.

- ambush your brother or sister with an unexpected slime attack.

- make a deal with your teacher. If your class averages over, say, 70% in an upcoming exam, the kids get to pour a bucket of slime on the teacher's head. And if your class averages less than 70%, the teacher gets to pour slime on your heads.

- paint your face in slime and wake your brother or sister early by positioning your face ten centimetres from theirs and saying 'Avocado', really loudly.

- hide a small amount of slime in a tissue or handkerchief, pretend to blow your nose, then show your friend or better, your grandmother, what you produced.

- coat your entire body in slime and walk down the main street with your arms out in front of you, repeating the word 'Zom-bie'.

zombie

Mr Schmittz

I don't really notice it at first. It creeps up on me like graveyard fog. I can't see it, but I feel it. The thing tickles my nose and gives me goosebumps, then BAM! It's in my ears and eyes and lungs, and all I want to do is shower and scrub my skin till it's raw. It's the worst thing I have ever smelt in my life.

At least, since the last time Mr Schmittz had a bad day.

Mr Schmittz is our school's longest serving teacher. Before that he was a scientist. Everybody loves him. If you try to say a bad word about Mr Schmittz in the playground, kids will actually make you take it back. He's 77 with a shiny, bald head, olive skin and a monocle – a single round eyepiece on a gold chain. His eyebrows are missing from a lab explosion back in 1967. Mr Schmittz is so excited about science that he kind of gets you excited, too. One time, he was so fired up that he stood up on his desk to sing us the periodic table song and got hit in the forehead by a ceiling fan, and kept right on teaching. That's how much he loves his job.

He's semiretired and only fills in for other teachers now. When you walk into the classroom and Mr Schmittz is there, you know it's going to be a fun day.

Lately, though, we've kind of started to dread it. I don't know if he's changed his diet and started drinking prune and baked-bean smoothies

Dried
fiGS
* Guaranteed
to make you
fart like a
champion

Mr Schmittz's SECRET weapon

for breakfast. Or maybe old age is just not agreeing with his digestive system. But something has gone very wrong inside Mr Schmittz.

Kids are burying their noses in the necks of their jumpers and creating gasmasks with their cupped hands. They're trying to do it politely, you can tell. No one wants to offend Mr Schmittz. He is at his desk listening to Sasha present her science project. I feel sorry for Sasha, standing so close to the source of the stink.

Mr Schmittz has A superpower THat he is unaware of.

She uses a miniature plastic cow to illustrate the effect of methane on global warming, and she looks a little green and woozy. Every 30 seconds or so, she turns her head away from Mr Schmittz and takes a large gulp of air, like a swimmer drawing breath.

She's trying not to make eye contact with anyone because if she does she will laugh, and everybody knows not to laugh when Mr Schmittz is having a bad day. The first time he 'broke wind' (as my nan would say) in class was about four months ago. It was a long, tight, dry ripping noise and the class fell into hysterics.

Mr Schmittz went mental. It's the only time I've ever heard him raise his voice, but he was so embarrassed and so angry that he gave us all recess detention. Since then we've tried to ignore the smell but it's getting difficult.

Mr Schmittz's bottom being taken away for testing.

The main problem is that it's winter and Mr Schmittz likes the windows closed on account of the pneumonia that almost killed him three years ago.

Sasha tells us about the molecular structure of methane and how it can be used as rocket fuel. She launches a hand-painted rocket into the air, adding blast-off sound effects.

I'm trying not to look at Jack, who's sitting next to me, because if I look at Jack I will laugh and if I laugh Mr Schmittz will go wild, and I would rather smell 10,000 of his farts than have him yell at us again. Somehow it's worse when someone who doesn't usually yell starts yelling. My mum can yell all day, every day, and I hardly even notice. But that one word, 'QUIET!', from Mr Schmittz has taken me months to get over.

But I have to get out of this room, or at least open a window. If I don't, I might need to have a nose transplant.

Sasha finishes her presentation and there are a few half-hearted claps. Only Mr Schmittz is enthusiastic. 'Well done, Sally! Lovely work.'

Sasha doesn't even bother correcting him on her name. She just grabs her assignment and scurries back to her desk. The air wobbles in front of her. Waves of hot stink radiate out to the rest of the room. Kids are physically pushed back in their chairs.

I put up my hand. 'Sir, can I please go to the bathroom?'

'Sorry, Todd. Lunch is only 15 minutes away. We have a few more presentations to get through. I'm sure you can hold it in. Who would like to go next?'

No one offers.

I reach over and, ever so quietly, inch the window open. There's a loud wood-on-wood squeal.

'Close the window, please, Todd,' says Mr Schmittz, squinting at me through his monocle.

'It's Tom. And I –'

'It's not summer.'

'No, but –'

'I'm sure you don't want to see me catch my death.'

'No, Mr Schmittz.'

'Then close the window.'

I squeeze my nose to the crack, suck in one almighty breath and shut the window.

Jack raises his hand. 'Sir?'

Mr Schmittz's watery eyes take on a serious look. Jack is the one kid who really gets up his nose.

'Yes, Jeremy,' says Mr Schmittz.

'It's Jack,' he says. 'Could I please go next?'

I know why Jack wants to go next. He loves the smell of farts. Not just his own. I mean, he *loves* the smell of his own. He thinks they smell like fresh, buttery popcorn with a hint of just-cut grass and chocolate frogs.

But he likes the smell of mine, too. He even likes his dad's. But how could Jack not be afraid of Mr Schmittz's rear-end toxic-waste facility? Greenpeace should campaign to have it corked.

'Certainly, let's see what you've got,' says Mr Schmittz.

Jack gives me a crooked grin, picks up his papier-mache volcano from the floor and walks up to the front of the classroom. I know Jack is going to say something funny about the smell and then Mr Schmittz will yell at us again. I can't let this happen.

Jack stands facing the class. I give him a warning look and he gently waves his hand towards his face to waft extra stench into his nostrils. Jonah Flem and Luca Kingsley snicker to my left, but I keep a straight face. Stella Holling makes a retching noise behind me and everyone turns to look at her.

'Is everything all right back there?' Mr

Schmittz asks, his gold monocle slipping from his eye.

'Yes, Mr Schmittz,' I say. 'Everything's fine.'

Stella leans down beneath her desk with a bulging brown lunch bag to her lips. She wipes her mouth with her wrist.

'What's going on?' Mr Schmittz asks.

'Nothing, sir,' I say, desperate not to rattle him.

'Mr Schmittz,' Jack says.

'Yes?'

'Do you . . . smell anything?'

Oh no. I hate Jack – I really do. How can he want to do this?

'No,' Mr Schmittz says, turning to Jack. 'Do you?'

We all watch Jack, who looks at me with a hint of a smile. 'Yes. Yes, I do,' he says.

Right on cue, Mr Schmittz lets one rip. It makes a gooey, runny sound. Mr Schmittz doesn't even seem to notice that he's the one who produced the noise. Jack breathes deep, as if he's on a meditation retreat, then launches into his presentation.

'I *was* going to demonstrate a live volcanic eruption, but . . .'

'Looks like you'll need a match to light that wick,' says Mr Schmittz.

'No, it's okay,' Jack tells him. 'I don't think we should light a match . . .'

'Of course we should,' Mr Schmittz says, opening the desk drawer. 'I'm looking forward to it.'

'No!' I call out. A spark right now could kill us all.

'I'm sorry? What was that?' Mr Schmittz asks, digging around in the drawer, searching for matches.

'Me. Todd. I mean Tom,' I say, standing from my seat. 'I agree with Jack. I don't think it's a good idea to light a match.'

'Why ever not?' asks Mr Schmittz.

'Well,' I say. 'Matches are dangerous and we should never play with matches.'

'But I'm an adult,' he says, taking a matchbox from the drawer.

'And . . .' says Jack, getting worried, too. 'There's a high fire danger today. It's a total fire ban. I saw it on the news.'

'But it's the middle of winter,' Mr Schmittz says. 'There's a frost out there.'

It does look kind of icy.

'Listen, Jeremy, if you haven't done your assignment correctly, stalling isn't going to stop me marking it. Let's get on with your presentation,' he says to Jack.

'But volcanoes are dangerous, Mr Schmittz!' I blurt. 'Remember Pompeii? And . . . and Krakatoa?'

Mr Schmittz chuckles. 'Jeremy's volcano does look impressive, but I hardly think it's going to burn the town down.'

'It's Jack,' Jack says.

Mr Schmittz bends over to light the volcano and his bowels fail him again. It's a low, mournful groan this time, like a dinosaur dying. It goes on for about seven seconds.

That does it. Kids crack up. They can't hold it in anymore. There are chortles, snorts and even a few guffaws. Mr Schmittz stands, his olive skin turning crimson with embarrassment. We've humiliated a 77-year-old man, our favourite teacher ... and it's all Jack's fault.

'QUIET!' he screams.

'He butt-burped,' Jonah Flem says, still laughing.

'I did NOT!' Mr Schmittz shrieks and his monocle pops out of his eye again. 'And, to prove it, I'll light this match. If there is methane present in this room, then –'

BOOOM!

In the split second before I close my eyes,

I see a fireball. I feel an enormous rush of hot air and then the spray of the sprinklers on my face.

I open my eyes and there is smoke, lots of it. Kids cough and panic. I head to the front of the classroom, searching for Mr Schmittz. Jack and a couple of other kids appear through the smoke. Jack's eyebrows are missing and Sasha is covered in ash. The sprinklers are soaking us. Our teacher is gone.

'Mr Schmittz!'

The classroom door flings open. 'Oh, my goodness. Everybody out!' Mrs Nicholl, one of the year four teachers, calls. 'Everyone out! Are you all okay?'

'Mr Schmittz!' I call.

The other kids rush for the door but I keep searching.

'Let's go, go, go!' says Mrs Nicholl, her eyes wild. She grabs me by the arm and leads me from the room.

'What about Mr Schmittz?'

'We'll find him,' she says. 'Are you okay? Are you injured?'

The other kids are led across the corridor and out into the playground, but I stop and look back into the classroom through the broken window. Chairs and tables are overturned and there is paper everywhere, some of it still burning. I scan the room but Mr Schmittz is nowhere to be seen. A mark on the floor up at the front of the room next to the teacher's desk catches my eye – a burnt, smoking patch on the lino, right where he had stood only moments ago.

I can see something shiny on the floor not far from the burnt patch. I sneak back into the room and pick my way through sprinkler spray and the twisted mess of furniture and books. I lean down and pick the thing up.

It's a monocle. The only thing that remains of my favourite teacher. The gold rim is hot and burns my fingers, but I keep hold of it and I put it up to my eye. The glass has smashed but I can still see through it.

Mr Schmittz, who gave his life to science, vaporised in a school science experiment. He was wiped out by a volcano. And his own bottom. I peer around the room, seeing the world the way he would have seen it through

that monocle, and I know one thing for sure. It sounds terrible, but I think Mr Schmittz would have liked the way he went. I really do. He went out with a bang.

Ten Reasons to Never EVER Sneak a Peek into The School Staffroom at Lunchtime

We were playing Truth or Dare at lunchtime and someone dared me to peek into the teachers' staffroom. I did, and I'll never recover. Here are ten reasons to avoid the staffroom at all costs.

I HATE all the students especially that TOM Weekly.

Me too. SHall we kill him?

1. You might see your mum in the staffroom with your teacher and they might both be wearing dark cloaks and sipping a fizzing, steaming brew, confirming your suspicions that they

are plotting to kill you by overloading you with homework, pointless jobs and making you eat healthy (read: poisonous) meals.

2. You might see two teachers kissing and then have to gouge out your own eyes.

3. You might catch them secretly digging a tunnel out of the shool to escape all the horrible students, and that might hurt your feelings a little bit.

4. You might see and smell what teachers eat for lunch, like flavoured tuna, with a fork, right out of the can.

5. They might be celebrating a teacher's birthday, and someone might see you at the door and invite you in to sing 'Happy Birthday' with them and give you a piece of cake. And it might be smoked corn and asparagus flavour with Spam icing, and they might expect you to eat it. And you may vomit all over the rest of the cake and be expelled. Or worse: not be expelled.

6. The cumulative stench of their instant-coffee breath might knock you out.

7. You might not have realised that it's World Disco Day, and the teachers have decided to hold a disco to raise money for kids in Cambodia, and you might see teachers practising their routine in sequined lycra outfits, which could stunt your growth and lead to lifelong mental disturbance.

8. You might not have realised that it's World Sloppy Food Day, when all teachers cook some sloppy food at home and bring it in to share. You might see teachers with straws, slurping sloppy food out of saucepans.

9. You might not have realised that it's World Wear Your Undies to Work Day and . . . well . . . you know . . .

10. You might see teachers laughing and sharing stories and eating and being normal. This could change your entire worldview and make you actually want to *become* a teacher!

Tooth Mine

'I'm going to have a convertible,' Jack says.

'I'm going to have a limousine,' I tell him.

'I'm going to have a convertible limousine.'

'Yeah, well, I'm going to have a convertible limousine with a cinema and a spa and a bowling alley in it,' I say.

'I'm going to have a bowling alley with nine cinemas and a 13-hole golf course.'

'Minigolf?'

'No, real,' he says.

'How are you going to fit a real golf course into a bowling alley that is inside a car?'

'My architect's working on it.'

Jack kicks a crushed lemonade can along the gutter with the tip of his holey-toed sneaker. We're walking up my street, heading home from the bus stop. I'm quiet for a bit, thinking about how cool it will be when we actually have the stuff we always dream about.

'I hate talking like this,' Jack says. 'It gets me all excited, then we can't do any of it. We need cash, and lots of it.' He kicks the can again.

'I know,' I say.

'Like, not a small amount. A *large* amount of cash,' Jack underlines, punting the can as he says *large*. 'Ow.'

'I know.'

'Like, more cash than Rupert Murdoch or Packer or Trump.'

'Absolutely.'

'More cash than there is in the world right now.'

'How's that even possible?'

'I don't know,' Jack says, 'but guys like us can make it possible. Some people complain about things being impossible but they shouldn't waste the time of guys like us who are already making stuff happen.'

We stop in front of my place. The grass in the front yard is up to my knees. I'm supposed to mow it but Mum won't pay me for it. She says it falls into the category of 'helping out around the house'.

'Maybe we could sink a mine in my yard,' I suggest, kicking at the ground.

'What?'

'A mine. That's how the government gets

cash. They let billionaires sink mines and then they sell all the stuff out of the ground to China.'

'But the only things buried in your backyard are broken toys. And . . . What was the name of your old dog?'

'Dennis.'

'And Dennis.'

'There might be other stuff. You never know till you start digging. I wonder how much a fracking rig costs,' I ask.

'Doesn't fracking leak gas into the water so you can light a match and set your tap water on fire?'

'I think so.'

'That'd be cool,' Jack says.

'Yeah. Mum'd get weird about it, though. I think she used to be a hippie.'

Jack and I dump our backpacks in the long grass and sit on the kerb.

'What else have we got?' I ask.

'I make plenty of natural gas, but after what

happened with Mr Schmittz, maybe we should rule that one out.'

'Yeah.' I bite my thumbnail.

Jack picks his nose.

'Don't pick your nose!'

'Why not?'

'I don't know. Hey, maybe we should sink a mine in your nose.'

'I've already got one up there,' Jack says. 'And I pull out, like, 100,000 dollars' worth of premium nuggets every day.'

'I wonder if China would be interested?'

Jack continues his mining project.

'What about body parts?' I suggest. 'You know, for people who need a replacement. On Mum's driver's licence she has to say whether she'll give away her kidneys when she dies, but what if they could get a nice, fresh, *living* kidney? That's got to be worth a bit.'

'What about hair?' Jack says. 'For old guys having hair transplants.'

'That's pretty good.' I get my maths
notebook out of my backpack and jot in the
back.

* Kidney
* Hair

'An arm?' I suggest. 'I wonder how much
you'd get for an arm . . . My left one really gets
in the way when I sleep. Sometimes I get pins
and needles and I can't feel it anymore and it's
so bad I think it's someone else's arm in the
bed and they're trying to rip my face off.'

* Kidney
* Hair
* Arm

I bite my thumbnail again and my front

teeth click together. 'What about teeth?'

'Teeth?'

I wiggle my top front tooth, then the ones around it. Then the bottoms.

'The tooth fairy pays five bucks a tooth, and I have maybe six baby teeth left, including the ones right up the back. That's 30 bucks.'

I quickly jot down the figures.

Jack's eyes dance and he starts wiggling his teeth like mad.

'I've got four, maybe five,' he says.

'That's a lot of cash just sitting there in our mouths doing nothing. Come inside.'

We head in to my house and go straight to the bathroom. We both open wide and try to count our baby teeth in the mirror. We think we might have $65 or even $70 in untapped assets.

'And when I stay at my nan's, the tooth fairy gives ten bucks,' I tell Jack.

today
only!

BODY
PARTS
for
sale

heart $10
arms $5 ea
legs $5 ea
kidney $7 ea
bum $5

'No way.'

'Yes way.'

'When are you staying there next?'

'What day is it?'

'Friday.'

'I could stay tonight.'

'Well, let's rip out a few of your teeth,' Jack says.

'I'll go get the pliers.'

I run to the laundry, excited. I can't believe Jack and I have come up with a business idea that's actually going to work. We are geniuses.

I find the head torch in the camping tub. I grab the pliers from the toolbox. I bolt back into the bathroom, flick on the torch and gaze into the mirror at all those beautiful, gleaming white gems inside my mouth.

'What's the point of teeth, anyway?' I ask Jack. 'Apart from eating.'

'They're annoying,' Jack says. 'Mum makes me brush mine, like, once a day.'

'I have to do mine twice,' I tell him.

'That's ridiculous,' Jack says. 'We should just rip 'em all out now. Imagine if you only had five teeth. You could brush them in 20 seconds rather than two minutes.'

'All we gotta do is bust 'em out.'

I hold up the pliers.

Jack and I look at them.

They're kind of old-looking and rusty, and when I try to pull them apart they squeal.

'I think they were Pop's. Maybe they need a bit of oil,' I say.

'Yeah.'

I go to the kitchen, bring back the canola oil spray and I spritz the pliers in the bathroom sink. I open and close them a few times and bright orange rust drips onto the white porcelain basin.

'What are we waiting for?' Jack says. 'Open up.'

Before I saw the pliers right up close, I

WHICH one first?

suspected they were old. But now I can see that the pincers are kind of jagged. They look like they must be pre-war. I'm not sure which war but it may have been one that was in the Bible.

'I wonder . . .'

'You wonder what?'

'I wonder if we could just wiggle them out instead?' I suggest.

'That'll take forever!'

'You want to go first?' I grab the brutal, rust-crusted implement and hold it up to Jack's face like I'm ready to operate.

His eyes widen and he steps back, almost falling into the bath. 'Maybe let's try the wiggling and see how we go.'

So Jack and I each find our loosest tooth and wiggle like crazy. We wiggle all afternoon, then we say goodbye and we wiggle all night. I stay at Nan's for the night, like we planned, but teeth are harder to pull out than I thought.

It takes me three whole days to work the first
tooth free, with very little blood loss. I wake
up Tuesday morning to five big bucks sitting
on my bedside table next to an empty glass of
water. The best part is that Mum can't take it
off me no matter how lazy I am. What kind of
a mother would steal tooth-fairy money?

I lie back on my bed, wondering if Jack
and I could franchise our tooth-mining idea
and sell it to kids all over the world. I use my
tongue to poke the smooth space where my
tooth once was. It tickles when I flick at the
loose threads of gum there.

At school Jack tells me he lost his tooth,
too. We are loaded, so we buy iceblocks and
milkshakes from the canteen at lunchtime.
We even buy lollies for other kids and
everyone is nice to us. We're finally getting
the respect we deserve. Life is pretty good.

We start working on our next teeth right
away. Over the next month, we each remove

three more teeth. It's like my face is an ATM. I press a few buttons and boom! Cash slides out from between my lips. I even time one of the teeth to 'fall out' at Nan's so that I get that tenner. With all these teeth missing, I'm starting to look like a jack-o'-lantern, which is cool because Halloween is next Friday.

The problem is, when money starts flowing that easily, you can get greedy. You really can. The teeth get harder to pull. And that's where Jack and I mess up.

I'm working on my next tooth for about four weeks and I'm getting worried. Jack is suddenly a tooth ahead of me and our cashflow has started to dry up.

'We've saved nothing for our dreams,' Jack says on the bus one morning. 'We've got nothing for the future. We've got to start putting some away.'

'Don't panic,' I tell him.

a beautiful
  equAtioN
_____

moutH - teetH
÷ tHe toothfairy
  = $

'I'm not panicking. But if you're just going
to spend everything we make ...'

'Yeah? How much have *you* got?'

'Four bucks!' Jack says. 'You?'

'This tooth is nearly out,' I tell him. 'I'll
have money soon.'

'You'd better, because I'm going to be a
billionaire, and you're either coming with me
or you're not.'

'Oh, I'm coming,' I tell him. 'I'll have the
money by tomorrow. Our first savings. We'll
start a bank account.'

'That's more like it,' he says. We seal the deal with a fist bump.

That day, it's Me v. Tooth. I wiggle it in class. I wiggle it on the way home. I wiggle it at soccer training. I wiggle it doing homework. I wiggle it in the shower. I wiggle it in bed and, finally, as sleep starts to take me, the tooth pops out. I nearly swallow it. I sit up, spit it into my palm and scream, 'Mum! I lost a tooth!'

She comes into my room, flicks on the lamp and says, 'Another one? Let me see.'

I show her. There's a bunch of blood and it feels like I have a Grand-Canyon-sized hole in my mouth. It hurts, but it's out and I suddenly have more money than Jack, and that is an unbelievable feeling.

'You've been losing so many teeth,' she says.

'I know. I wish it'd stop.' I hold my cheek like I'm in pain.

'Well, we'd better leave this out for the tooth fairy, I suppose. If you keep losing teeth I'll have to get a second job.'

I laugh and blood dribbles down my chin.

Mum plucks a tissue out of her sleeve and mops it up.

She looks at the tooth, turns it over in her palm, then stands and holds it up to the lamp light, inspecting it closely.

'Thomas?' she says, turning the tooth over in her hand.

This worries me. I'm pretty sure my mother is, secretly, a spy. Sometimes she knows that I've done something wrong before I even do it.

'Yes, Mum?' I say.

'I smell a rat.'

'Maybe it's Rarnalda,' I say, making a joke about my pet rat.

'Tilt your head back.'

'But I –'

'Open your mouth!' she snaps, sticking two fingers in my gob and prying my jaw wide.

'How many teeth have you lost in the last couple of months?' she asks.

'Ot any,' I say, by which I mean 'not many', but it's kind of hard to speak when someone's fingers are jammed in your mouth.

'Tom?'

'Um . . . fee?' I say. By which I mean 'three'.

'Five!' Mum says. 'I can see the gaps.' She pulls out her fingers and wipes them on my pyjamas. 'This is the fifth tooth in two months. Why is that, Tom?'

'Just unlucky?' I suggest, shrugging. 'Kids grow up before you know it.'

'Jack's mum said he'd lost a few teeth lately, too. Is that true?'

'Not sure,' I say, trying to yawn. 'I'm really tired. I might –'

'I don't think this is a baby tooth,' Mum says. 'This is an adult tooth.'

She holds it up to me. It does seem kind of big.

'You've lost an adult tooth, Tom. Did you *pull* this tooth out?'

'Um.'

'Honestly, Tom. Was this about money?' She stands and looks down at me. 'I hope you saved a lot. Replacing adult teeth is a very expensive business.'

She snaps off my lamp. 'We'll talk in the morning.' She leaves my room and closes my door a little too firmly. I sit alone in the dark. The gap where the tooth was now howls with pain. I feel stupid and greedy and sad that my promising mining career is over already. I'm also worried that Jack is going to end up a billionaire and I won't.

'Mum, does this mean the tooth fairy's not coming? . . . Mum?'

the tooth fairy doesn't
do ADULT teeth (who knew?)

15 Things You Won't Hear Your Mother Say Anytime Soon

1. 'Let's do something fun.'

2. 'Oh, what a cute rat you've found. Of course you can keep her and name her and build a hutch for her under your bed. Can I get Rarnalda something to eat?'

3. 'Fifty-two per cent on your maths test! That means you got more right than you got wrong! Well done! Let's go buy a milkshake to celebrate.'

4. 'Life's too short. Why don't we just have fairy floss, toffee apples and lemonade for dinner?'

5. 'Can you invite Jack around more often? I love waking to the sweet sound of you two playing video games at 5 o'clock on a Sunday morning.'

6. 'Darling, weeing on the toilet seat is just part of being a boy. I don't mind wiping the back of my legs when I stand up.'

7. 'Of course you can have my PIN number. It's 3724.'

8. 'Of course I don't mind that you like a girl at school more than you like me.'

9. 'Of course it's okay that you smashed a lamp over your sister's head and then stuffed marshmallows up her nose and farted on her.'

10. 'I'd *love* to watch a Star Wars movie marathon with you this weekend.'

11. 'No, I don't mind you cutting the heads off your sister's porcelain dolls. I thought they were creepy, too.'

12. 'Of course I don't mind you taking money from my wallet without asking. What's mine is yours, Sweetheart.'

13. 'I love it when you answer back. I think it's wonderful to have healthy debate over every decision that needs to be made.'

14. 'Wow, I love what you're doing with those boogers on the wall next to your bed. It's so nice and rough. I wonder if we could use that as a cheese grater?'

15. 'What a great idea, you using the front garden as a toilet. It's good for the azaleas and who cares what the neighbours think?'

HoNey, would you mind kicking your football THROUGH the window? It's HOT in here!

Sore

It's 4.37, Tuesday afternoon. Jack and I are standing in the doorway of Bunder's Fish Shop, staring at Brent Bunder, who is behind the counter chopping chips. Brent's the biggest, meanest kid in our school. He stops chopping, looks up at us, shakes his head and says, 'Idiots.'

Jack and I smile and head inside. The word 'idiots' is like a handwritten invitation from Brent.

'What do youse want?' he asks. But he knows. And he knows that we know he knows. So Jack and I are grinning like madmen.

'Just some chips,' Jack says.

'Five bucks' or ten bucks' worth?' Brent asks.

'Why not ten?' Jack says, which is crazy because we've never even *seen* ten dollars' worth of chips before. We stand at the counter, grinning at Brent, who holds the big chip-chopping knife. It doesn't scare us, though. Brent Bunder doesn't need a chip-chopping knife to scare me and Jack. He could injure us with his pinkie or his big toe if he wanted to.

'Give me your money,' Brent says.

'Well, that's the thing,' Jack says. 'We don't exactly –'

give ME
Your MoNey

BRENT BUNDER
has A
beautiful
Smile.

'Get lost then,' Brent grunts and goes back to chopping.

Jack and I keep smiling. It's all part of the routine. Every Tuesday afternoon when Brent's mum does Pilates and his dad sneaks out to bet on horses, Brent works in the chip shop and we come in and ask for hot chips. Brent asks us for cash. We tell him we don't have any. He tells us to get lost. Then we ask him if he needs any work done around the shop.

'You need any work done around the shop?' Jack asks.

Brent slams down the chip-chopping knife, leaving it sticking out of the big wooden chopping block.

'Matter of fact,' he says, 'I've got something better for you today.'

'What?' I ask, dreading what he'll make us do this time. Once he made us go to the damp, dark potato storage room downstairs and haul nine massive bags of potatoes up the stairs in exchange for about 80 cents' worth of chips. Another time we had to fish all the crusty bits of batter and dim sim out of the deep-fryer for a dollar fifty's worth.

But Bunder's chips are so good you'd do just about anything for a handful of them. At Bunder's, they don't just take a plastic bag of chips from who knows where out of the freezer and pour them into the deep-fryer. No way. The Bunders are chip professionals. They chop chips from potatoes – *actual* potatoes that grew on a farm somewhere, at some stage, within a few thousand kilometres of here. Sometimes you even get a bit of dirt on your chip which, for hot chipologists like me and Jack, is gold.

It's these little touches that make Bunder's the best hot chip restaurant in the world. (Restaurant is probably taking it a bit far. There's only one seat and it's broken IKEA plastic. It sits in front of the old Space

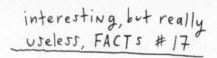

interesting, but really
useless, FACTS #17

Bunder's CHIPS come from
actual reAl potatoes !
(crazy, right !?)

Invaders arcade game that's been there since about 1932. Jack and I fight over the seat every time we go in there. In fact, I think we might have broken it in the first place.)

'I want each of you to eat a chip that's been dipped in my sore,' Brent says.

I swallow hard and I'm just about to say, 'What sore?' when Jack jumps in and says, 'Done!' He holds out his hand to shake with Brent Bunder.

Brent goes to grab Jack's hand with one of his bone-crushing shakes, but I rip Jack's hand back just in time.

'Show us your sore,' I say.

'Don't listen to him,' Jack says. 'We'll do it.' And he holds out his hand again.

This time Brent grabs it and I can hear bones in Jack's hand breaking.

The deal is done.

'We haven't even seen the sore!' I snap at Jack.

'Doesn't matter,' Jack says. 'It's ten dollars' worth of chips. That'll feed us for the rest of our lives. How bad could the sore be?'

We look at Brent and he smiles. Brent doesn't often smile. In fact, I don't know if I've ever seen him smile, but he's smiling now. This worries me. Jack puts on a brave face but I can tell that it worries him, too.

A cockroach scuttles up the white-tiled wall and a blowfly buzzes around Brent's head, landing on his face. He swats at it but misses and slaps himself across the cheek.

I don't feel that hungry anymore when I

think about eating a chip dipped in Brent's
sore. And I don't like the word 'dipped',
either. I mean, how deep is this thing if you
can actually *dip* a chip into it? I can imagine
wiping a chip on a sore or *scraping* the surface,
but *dipping* makes it sound so . . . deep.

'You want to see it now?' Brent asks. 'Or
you want to wait till the chips are cooked?'

'Now!' I say.

'We'll wait!' Jack says.

I growl at Jack. He growls back.

'All right, we'll wait,' I grunt.

So Brent goes to work. He scoops up the
mother lode of chips and throws them into
the basket, lowering it into the oil with one of
his enormous hands.

Jack and I sit on the broken seat, one bum-
cheek each.

'That's heaps more than he usually
gives us,' I whisper to Jack nervously.

'I know. It's awesome,' Jack says.

'Doesn't it worry you?' I ask.

'Why would I worry about eating more chips?'

'Because the bigger the job we do, the more chips he gives us. That's double the amount we got for cleaning the oil, and that took us two hours.'

'So?' Jack asks dumbly.

'So, if all we've got to do is eat a chip that's been dipped in a sore . . .' I say.

He thinks about it for a bit then says, 'What?'

'It must be a pretty bad sore!' I hiss, loud enough for Brent to hear me over the crackle and spit of the fryer. He turns and looks at us. I smile to suggest to Brent that everything's hunky-dory.

'He doesn't even look like he's got a sore,' Jack whispers. 'He's probably bluffing. Maybe he just likes us now. Maybe he admires us for being brave enough to just show up and ask

him for free chips. What other kids in our
year would be stupid enough to do that?'

'I s'pose.'

'And maybe he thinks we're his friends?
I mean, what other friends has that big freak
got?' Jack whispers.

I try to think who Brent's friends are but
I can't think of any. He just wanders around
the playground scaring people. When he
walks across the oval it's like Moses parting
the Red Sea. Kids scatter. No one even wants
to go *near* Brent in case he decides to clobber
them. This sort of makes me sad.

I watch Brent, who has his back to us,
bending over at the deep-fryer. His gigantic
ears stick out from his head like satellite dishes
scanning other galaxies for potential friends,
and I feel really sorry for him.

'True,' I say. 'We're probably his only
buddies.'

Brent heaves the chip basket out of the

fryer and clips it to the rim, allowing the oil
to drip off. I can smell them now. Freshly
chopped, freshly fried.

'There are so *many* of them,' Jack says.

'Crazy,' I say.

'Now are you happy I did the deal?'

We move up to the counter. Brent grins
at us. I grin back. He turns the chips out
of the basket onto fresh greaseproof paper.
It's an *Everest* of chips. It looks more like *20*

dollars' worth. Jack and I watch, eyes wide, as Brent shakes salt all over them. Jack laughs in disbelief. Saliva spills down my chin and I wipe it off with the cuff of my school jumper.

Brent wraps the chips up into a cone, leaving the top open for easy access. He pours what looks like a litre of vinegar into the cone and my eyes start to water from the smell of the vinegar and salt and all the steam and the feeling of warmth from knowing that we have a friend who works in the best chip shop in Kings Bay, and that he gives us chips even when he doesn't really have a sore to dip them in.

Brent holds them out to us. Jack and I reach for the package. Just as my fingertips scrape that beautiful, hot, vinegar-soaked paper and my stomach lets out a Jurassic groan, Brent pulls back the chips and says, 'Oh. That's right.'

Jack and I look at him.

'The sore,' he says.

Jack laughs and points at Brent. 'You don't really have a sore, do you?'

Brent laughs and points back at Jack. Then I laugh.

Brent sets the chips aside, out of reach. Jack and I watch them, like my dog Bando watches his bowl when I make him sit for a few seconds before he has dinner.

Brent starts rolling up the left sleeve of his school jumper. There doesn't seem to be a scab on his arm at all. There are a few really ugly moles and more hair than most fully grown men have on their entire bodies, but no scab. I look at Brent, knowing that he's kidding us. But he keeps rolling up that sleeve till it's pulled tight around his brick of a bicep, revealing a bandaged elbow.

'What happened?' I ask.

'Footy,' he says. 'On the weekend.' He flicks open the elastic and metal clip on the bandage and starts to unravel it. He carefully unspools the bandage, letting it fall to the chopping board, right next to the freshly chopped chips. This seems like a health hazard to me, but I decide not to mention it.

As the layers unravel, I see that there's an area of bandage right on the point of the elbow that seems to be stained yellow. As each layer falls to the chopping board, the area becomes yellower and yellower until just the sight of it makes my stomach turn.

I have never seen anything that yellow. Ever. Butter is not that yellow. Small ducks are not that yellow. The sun is not that yellow. Then the final layer falls away and I see something yellower still.

Brent Bunder's sore.

The fluoro lights flicker. The buzzing fly lands on the sore and Brent swats it, squishing the fly into the yellow moistness, then flicking it off.

officially THE grossest tHing I've EVEr seen!

I turn away. 'That looks really . . . deep,'
I say, covering my mouth.

'Yeah,' Brent says, laughing a bit. 'It hurts.
Their second-rower's stud sank right in. You
could see through to the bone, eh.'

'Right,' I say, trying not to be sick, which
is what I usually do when I hear about human
bones being visible through flesh.

'We'd better get this over with,' Brent
says, looking at his watch. 'It's nearly five and
my dad'll be back soon. He'll blow up if he
knows I'm giving chips away.'

He reaches for a couple of chips from the

top of the cone. He dips one right into that yellow pit of a sore, as if it were the runny yolk of a fried egg. He sucks in a sharp breath. I bet he can feel the salt and vinegar deep inside the sore. My face twists, imagining the pain.

He holds the chip out to me. It's about five centimetres long with yellow ooze dripping from it.

'Jack'll go first,' I say.

'*What?*' Jack explodes. 'I don't even *like* chips.'

'Yes you d—'

'Are you babies going to keep your end of the deal or what?'

We look up at him. He is sweaty and serious.

I look at the chip. Some of the yellow stuff drips onto the counter and Brent wipes it up with one of his sausage fingers. He offers the chip to Jack.

'I'm not eating it,' Jack says.

Brent utters a low, animal growl.

'It's disgusting!' I tell him.

'You boys made a deal. Are you backing out of a deal?'

I lick my lips. Two minutes ago, my mouth was swimming in saliva. Now it's the Simpson Desert. I know I can't eat the chip, but I know I can't say 'no' to Brent Bunder.

'How about we make another deal?' I say, forcing a smile. 'We'll drag nine bags of potatoes up from downstairs *and* clean all the junk out of the deep-fryer . . . but we don't have to eat the chip.'

Brent thrusts his enormous hand out over the counter and grabs me by the neck of my jumper. He's pretty fast, Brent, for a big guy. I'm kind of choking now. Jack backs off and I'm hoping he's not going to run, which is what he would usually do in a situation like this.

'Eat the chip!' Brent says, revealing his missing tooth and breathing fish-breath on me. He moves the chip towards my mouth as if he's feeding a baby. The chip is about five centimetres from my mouth and I'm going to be sick. I have quite a weak stomach when it comes to things like this, I really do.

Three centimetres.

I don't *want* to vomit but he keeps moving the chip towards me.

Two centimetres.

I can smell the sharp tang of the yellow stuff from the sore.

One centimetre.

I can't really see the chip clearly anymore. It's pretty much in my mouth when I see something move out of the corner of my eye. It's Jack. He's launched himself across the counter and swipes at the chips.

'Oi!' Brent lets go of me and flies at Jack, but Jack's too quick. Brent rips the cone away from Jack. The newspaper tears and chips explode from the package. Jack scoops up two piping hot handfuls, stuffs them into the pockets of his school shorts, and bolts for the door, shouting, 'Ruuun!'

I snatch a handful of chips and turn but Brent grabs the back of my jumper. He pulls it. He's reeling me in as if I were a fish.

I panic and twist and turn until I hear the jumper rip. It tears right up the back and then I'm out of the jumper and running for the door, leaving Brent lying sprawled over the chopping board.

'You two are dead!' he screams.

As I hit the doorway, I run smack into Brent's dad, almost knocking myself out. Mr Bunder is built like a fridge.

'What are you doin'?' he demands, but I squeeze past him and head into the main street where there is bright sunlight and regular humans and safety. We run for our lives.

We do not go back to Bunder's Fish Shop the following Tuesday afternoon. We do not go within 20 metres of Brent Bunder for the next month, even though he's in our class. We spend every lunchtime in the library reading books about kung-fu and taekwondo and a little-known martial art called we-so-scared. Brent prowls past the library window 20 times each lunch hour like an agitated grizzly, just waiting for his chance.

We got away with a few chips that day but I had my fist squeezed so tight they were like mashed potato by the time I ate them. Now Jack and I have made a vow never to eat hot chips again.

But I don't know how long it'll last. Bunder's just smells so good, and some days when I'm feeling very poor and very hungry, I regret not eating that one chip – I really do. And I wonder if Brent would let us make it up to him next time he gets a really bad sore from footy. I don't like to admit it but every Monday morning I keep a lookout for Brent, hoping that he'll come to school with a bandage on his arm. Then I'll know it's only about 31 hours before it's Tuesday afternoon at 4.37 and maybe, just maybe, Brent might dip a chip in exchange for ten dollars' worth. I'd eat it for sure next time. Wouldn't you?

Story Starters

Writing stories is fun but difficult. Getting started is the toughest part. I have a thousand beginnings of stories in my notebooks so I thought I'd share a few in case they inspire you to write your own 'My Life' story.

Here are three things I have learned from writing short stories:

1. It's easier and more fun if you use things that happen to you in your own life and then supercharge it with your imagination.

2. Keep it simple. Don't try to stuff a whole chunky novel into 500 words.

3. It gets confusing if you have too many characters or settings. It's better to tell a simple story than to set up 36 characters and 15 locations.

Here are some lines to get you started:

- 'You try living on a pension,' said Nan, pulling on her black balaclava.

- My grandfather has magnificently large earlobes. They are elephantine, gargantuan and splendiferous. And, one time, they saved my life.

- Jack and I have started a band. It's not like any other band you've ever heard. It's edgy, out there, ahead of its time. See, we can't really play any instruments. And we can't sing. But we can . . .

- 'I dare you to go in . . .'

- Jack's dad thinks he's the new Bear Grylls. Jack's dad is not the new Bear Grylls. Jack's dad is a maniac and we are going to die.

- Jack and I are pretty good at breaking stuff so we've decided we're going to break a world record.

- 'I know this is a totally weird question but does your poo ever talk to you? Sometimes, when I get up in the middle of the night to go to the toilet I sit down and I hear this little voice from down below . . .'

And a few title ideas:
- Vampire Nits v. Alien Nits

- Death by Mouldy Sandwich

- Scab Farm

- World's Weirdest Cat

If you write a funny short story and want to see it in my next book or on my website, send it to TheTomWeekly@gmail.com and I'll get right back to you.

I Remember . . .

Sometimes the stuff that happens in real life is crazier than anything you could make up. I always start my stories with something that actually happened and then mash it up with my imagination. It's a pretty fun way to write. If you want to give it a try, set a timer for five minutes and write a list of as many memories as you can, like I have below. Remember, don't stop writing for the whole five minutes. Don't worry about spelling or neatness. Just get it down. And . . . go.

I remember . . .

- when my sister tried to make me eat Vegemite off her big toe.

- trying to frame my dog for a crime he did not commit.

- attempting to eat 68 hot dogs in ten minutes.

- wearing an ice-cream container on my head to avoid being attacked by magpies.

- the time I, Tom Weekly, became a dog kisser.

- my nan being in a back-alley brawl with Jack's nan.

- Mr Skroop chopping up my football and posting it into my letterbox.

- running a mini freak show in the school playground and thinking it would make me rich.

- the time Raph Atkins' dog ate the last two Jagrofest birds on earth.

- being attacked at KidsWorld by a dangerous gang of vigilante toddlers armed with nappies.

When your five minutes are up,
choose your favourite memory and
set the timer for another five minutes.
Write out that memory in detail
but mash in lots of stuff that didn't
happen, too, to make it funnier and
weirder and grosser. Voila! You have
the beginnings of your own 'My Life'
story.

ice - cream
man

Acknowledgements

Special thanks to:

Amber Melody, Hux and Luca, for being my constant companions and my first readers and listeners. Gus Gordon for being a good human and a kooky collaborator. Sophie Hamley, Paul McMahon, Claire Atkins and Raph Atkins for their creativity and support. My teachers, Susanne Bannister, Bill Spence, Les Ridgeway, Belinda Austin and John McKinlay, teachers who valued creativity and nurtured mine. And the team at Random House Australia – Zoe Walton, Brandon VanOver, Bronwyn O'Reilly, Astred Hicks, Dot Tonkin, Julie Burland, Zoe Bechara, Angela Duke, Caroline Ayling and Sarana Emerton, who support me through every step of creating and sharing these stories.

Thanks to Ruby Barker for coming up with the brilliant title, My *Life & Other Massive Mistakes*. She left the idea as a blog comment here: http://www.tristanbancks. com/2014/05/my-life-3-book-title.html. Thanks to the schools and groups who have brainstormed 'Cranky Dad Syndrome' and 'Stella Holling: Sugar Rush' with me at live events: St Paul's Grammar School, Leichhardt PS, Westmead PS, Blackheath PS, Gosford East PS, St John the Baptist PS, AIS Singapore, Overseas Family School Singapore, UWC SEA East, Singapore American School, Tara Anglican School for Girls, Wooloowin SS, Shorncliffe SS, Holy Cross PS, Jubilee PS, St Ita's PS, Living Faith Lutheran PS, Ipswich StoryArts Festival, Silkstone SS, Bethany Lutheran PS, Toogoolawah SS, Redeemer Lutheran College, Chapel Hill SS, Charlestown PS, Gladstone Central SS, Star of the

Sea Catholic PS, Gladstone South SS, Mount Larcom SS, Tannum Sands SS, Alkimos Baptist College, Holy Family PS Indooroopilly, Brooklyn PS, Cowan PS, Pottsville Beach PS, Cammeray PS, Gleneagles Secondary College, Yarrilee SS, Sandy Strait SS, St Matthew's Catholic PS Cornubia, Lindisfarne Anglican Grammar, St Francis Xavier PS, Auburn West PS, Umina PS, Woollahra PS, Leura PS, Oatlands District HS, New Town HS, Xavier College Burke Hall, Landsborough SS, Kenilworth CC, Bli Bli SS, Mt Creek SS, Chevallum SS, Our Lady of the Rosary Catholic PS, Gympie East SS, Macgregor SS, Chinchilla SS, Graceville SS, Moggill SS, Stretton SS, Churchie, Camira SS, St Joseph's PS, Nudgee Junior College, Woodcrest SS, Bulimba SS, All Hallows' School, The Springfield Anglican College, Kelvin Grove State College, Somerset Celebration of Literature participants, 2014 Bardon Young Writers Week participants, 2014 LitVids book trailer-making workshop participants, 2014 Newcastle Writers Festival workshop participants and 2014 SLQ Story Lab participants.

Thanks to the following for submitting their CDS ideas: Alim, Auburn, Sage, Paco, Jess, Lucy, Ivy, Archie, Sofia, Patrick, Tia, Shruti, Cassandra, Ceren, Melih, Ershad, Mohammad, Donia, Elif, Ally, Mariam, Malack, Lachlan, Charlotte, Anjali, Johnathan, Stacey, James, Jackson, Natasha A, Tristan, Gayathiri, Beth, Milo, Tara, Alicia, Brody, William, Alex, Hamish, Tahlia, Amanda, Jack, Jordan, Jacey, Breyer, Samuel, Khyl, Emmzy G, Angus (sausages in the remote idea!), Rosie, Eliza, Scarlett, Khyl D, Kade, Davara, James, Hamish, Tara, Jack, Henry, Nicholas, Zach, Chloe, Jordan,

Liron, Holly, Ayan, Elliot, Emmzy, Oliver, Rebecca, Jarn,
Kyle, Danny, Fynnlay, Ryan, Hux, Dominic, Tehya, Bailey,
Luca, Kohl, Georgia, James, Ryan, Broken-arm Emma, Mat,
Jacob, Eliana, Kyle, Brody, Carly, Mason, Alec, Brandon,
Mads, Kashalyn, Xavier, Tayla, Taliya, Chris, Ariana, Christos,
Vincent, Michael, Oliver, Shruti, Nate, Daniel, Edward,
Owen, Baxter, William, Nick, Shaun, Andrew, Lexie, Kyle,
Cooper, Levi, Reuben and Deeksha.

And a big thanks to my immature Twitter and
Facebook buddies, as well as the crowd at Byron Bay
Writers Festival who helped brainstorm the innovative
weapons and geriatric escape techniques used in 'The Great
Escape'.

Tristan Bancks is a children's and teen author published in Australia and the US. His background is in acting and filmmaking. His books include the *My Life* series, *Two Wolves* and *Mac Slater Coolhunter*. *My Life & Other Stuff I Made Up* has been nominated for BILBY and KOALA children's choice awards. Tristan is excited by the future of storytelling and inspiring others to create. Find out more and chat to Tristan at www.tristanbancks.com.

Gus Gordon has written and illustrated over 70 books for children. He writes books about motorbike-riding stunt chickens, dogs that live in trees and singing on rooftops in New York. His picture book *Herman and Rosie* was a 2013 CBCA Honour Book. Gus loves speaking to kids about illustration, character design and the desire to control a wiggly line. Visit Gus at www.gusgordon.com

MY LIFE
AND OTHER STUFF
I MADE UP

Have you ever been kissed by a dog? Ever
had to eat Vegemite off your sister's big toe?
Have you had a job delivering teeth? Has a
bloodthirsty magpie ever been out to get you?
Ever woken up to discover that everything
hovers? And have you eaten 67 hot dogs in ten
minutes?

I have. I'm Tom Weekly. This book is full of
my stories, jokes, cartoon characters, ideas for
theme park rides and other stuff I've made
up. It's where I pour out whatever's inside my
head. It gets a bit weird sometimes, but that's
how I roll.

Available now

MY LIFE
AND OTHER STUFF THAT
WENT WRONG

Is your grandpa super-angry? Has your nan
ever tried to climb Mt Everest? Have you
started your own playground freak show? And
have you ever risked your life to save your pet
rat from certain destruction?

I have. I'm Tom Weekly and this is my
life. Inside the covers of this book you'll read
lots of weird-funny-gross stories and learn
the secret of my strangest body part. But I
guarantee that won't freak you out as much as
the story of how Stella Holling, a girl who's
been in love with me since second grade,
tricked me into kissing her.

Available now

MAC SLATER, COOLHUNTER 1: THE RULES OF COOL

Mac's just crashed the latest prototype of his flying bike in front of practically the whole school. So when the creators of Coolhunters approach him and tell him he's an Innovator, Mac thinks they're crazy.

They offer Mac a trial. He'll vlog all the cool stuff coming out of Kings Bay for a week. If he wins he'll travel the world, uncovering stuff he loves and reporting it via Coolhunters, a massive online space dedicated to the coolest things on earth.

But hunting cool ain't easy. Mac's opponent, Cat DeVrees, wants the gig real bad, and she'll do just about anything to get it.

Available now

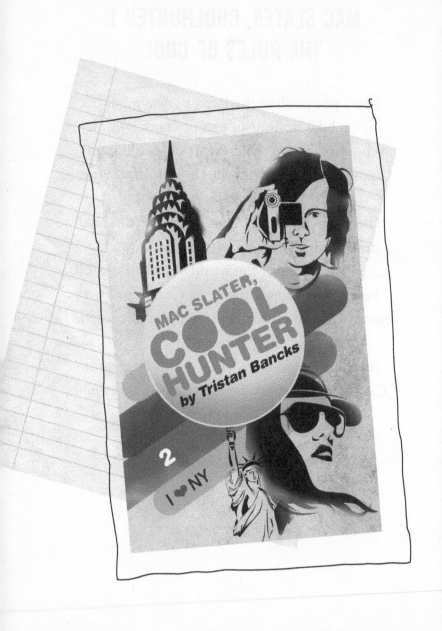

MAC SLATER, COOLHUNTER 2:
THE RULES OF COOL

MAC SLATER, COOLHUNTER 2: I ♥ NY

Imagine being offered an all-expenses-paid
trip to New York City! It seemed like an
impossible dream for Mac and his best friend,
Paul. But they've just become coolhunters
for a massively popular webspace and Mac
is beyond excited. The catch: he has to find
the Next Big Thing in NYC – or be sent
home. Mac soon makes friends with Melody,
an inventor with super-cool skates, who takes
him to The Hive. It's an old boatshed where
innovative kids are creating transport, sneakers
and computer apps that are way more cutting
edge than anything you can buy. And the Hive
kids are about to test an invention that could
change the world.

Mac's boss at Coolhunters is desperate for him
to spill the beans, but Melody has sworn Mac
to secrecy. He's found the coolest thing in
NYC and he's not allowed to tell a soul!
Friends or fame. Which would you choose?

Available now

TWO WOLVES

*'Gripping and unpredictable,
with a hero you won't forget.'*
– **John Boyne, author of**
The Boy in the Striped Pyjamas

One afternoon, police officers show up at Ben
Silver's front door. Minutes after they leave, his
parents arrive home. Ben and his little sister,
Olive, are bundled into the car and told they're
going on a holiday. But are they?
It doesn't take long for Ben to realise that his
parents are in trouble. Ben's always dreamt of
becoming a detective – his dad even calls him
'Cop'. Now Ben gathers evidence and tries to
uncover what his parents have done.
The problem is, if he figures it out, what does
he do? Tell someone? Or keep the secret and
live life on the run?

Available now